FAR OUT
CLASSIC STORIES

STONE ARCH BOOKS
a capstone imprint

D0128815

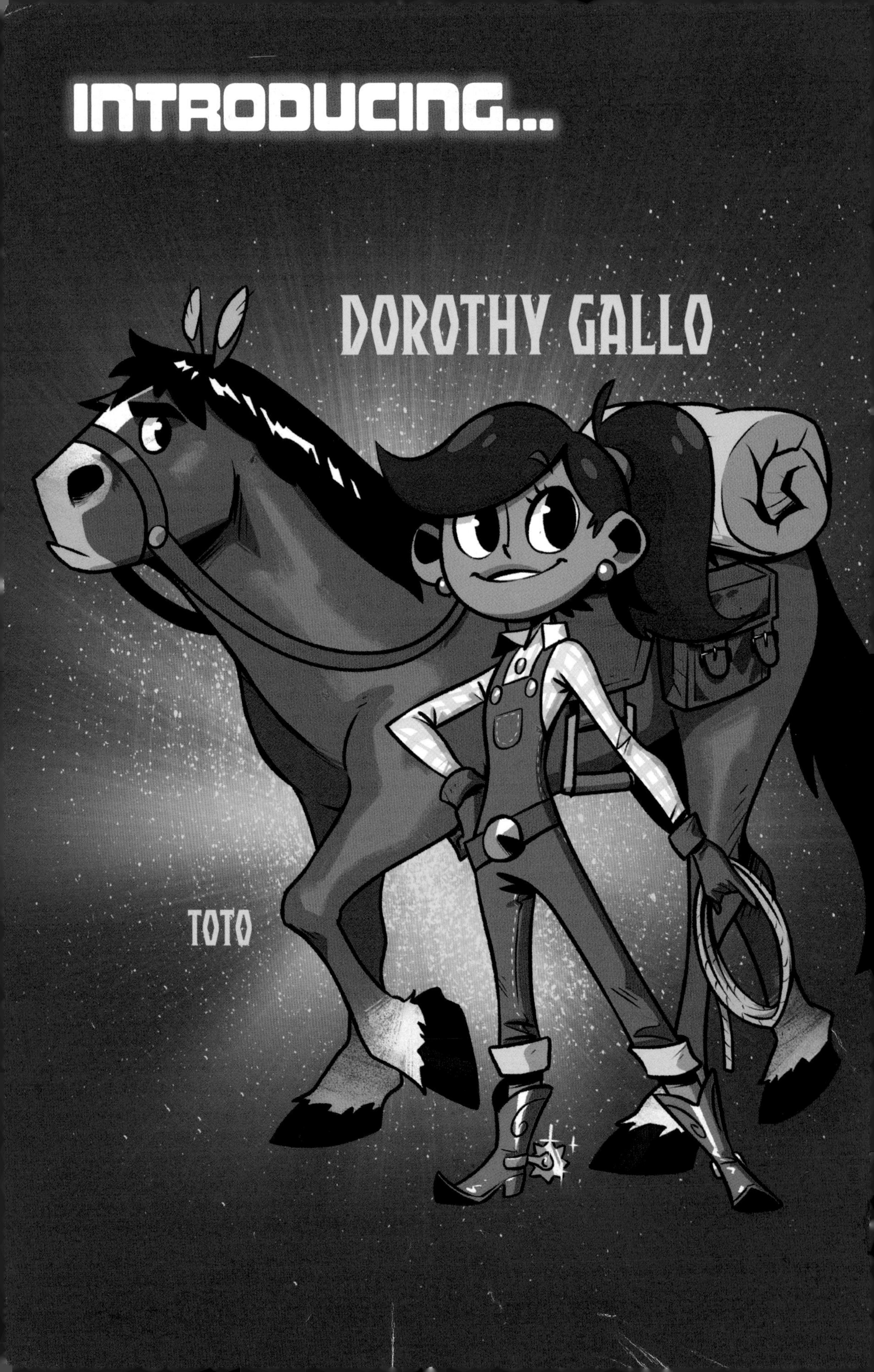
INTRODUCING...
DOROTHY GALLO
TOTO

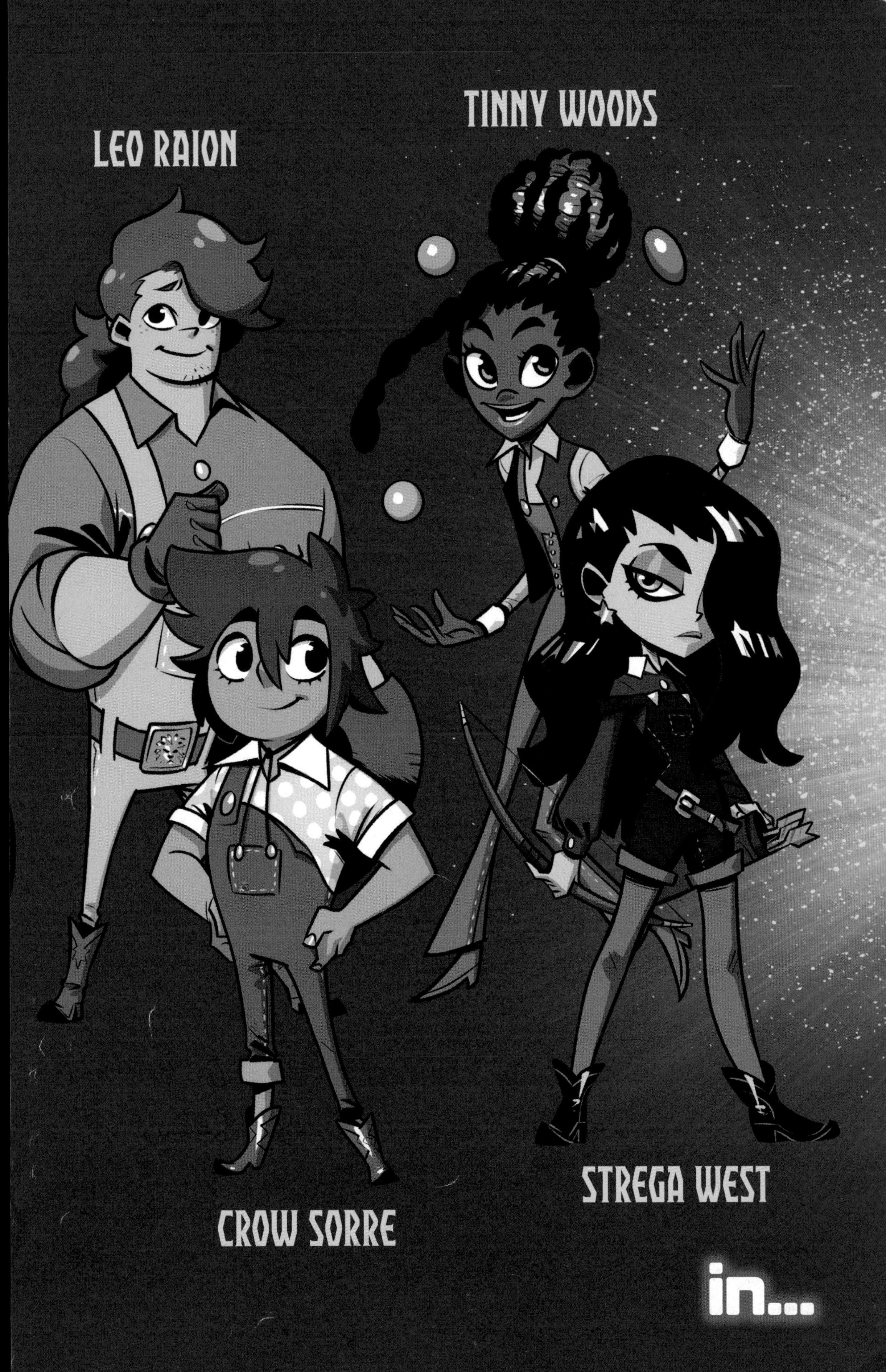
LEO RAION
TINNY WOODS
STREGA WEST
CROW SORRE
in...

Far Out Classic Stories is published by
Stone Arch Books,
an imprint of Capstone.
1710 Roe Crest Drive
North Mankato, Minnesota 56003
www.capstonepub.com

Library of Congress Cataloging-in-
Publication Data is available on the
Library of Congress website.
ISBN: 978-1-4965-8690-2 (hardcover)
ISBN: 978-1-4965-9195-1 (paperback)
ISBN: 978-1-4965-8691-9 (ebook PDF)

Summary: Cowgirl Dorothy and her
horse, Toto, are riding to see the Wiz
Kid! The entertainer is auditioning new
acts for his Emerald Circus, and Dorothy
and her friends Tinny, Crow, and Leo,
hope they can impress him with their
talents. But when Dorothy's lucky silver
spurs go missing, will she still be able to
perform her best?

Designed by Hilary Wacholz
Edited by Abby Huff
Lettered by Jaymes Reed

Printed and bound in the USA.
PA99

FAR OUT CLASSIC STORIES

THE SILVER SPURS OF OZ

A GRAPHIC NOVEL

BY ERICA SCHULTZ

ILLUSTRATED BY OMAR LOZANO

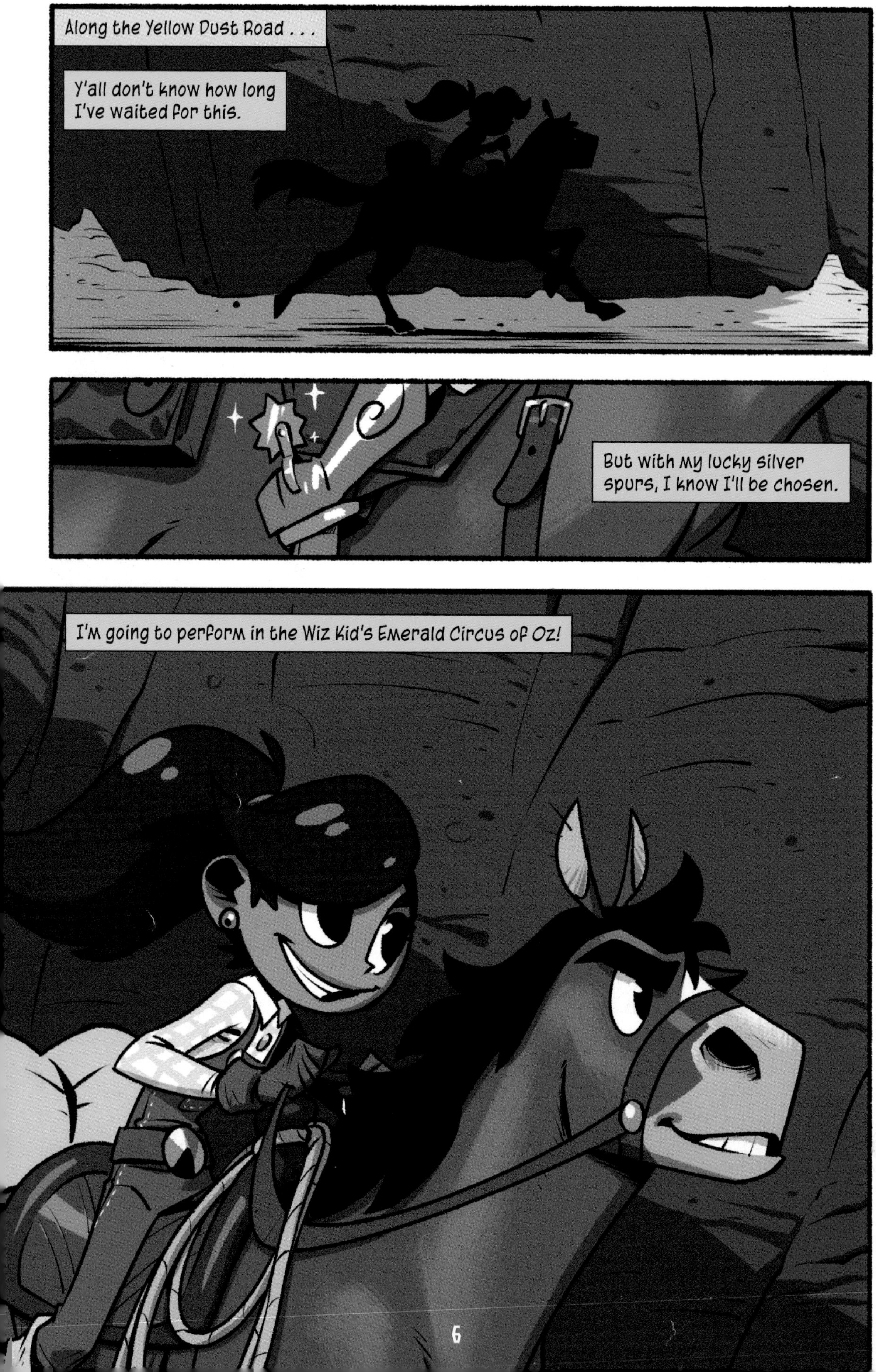
Along the Yellow Dust Road . . .
Y'all don't know how long I've waited for this.
But with my lucky silver spurs, I know I'll be chosen.
I'm going to perform in the Wiz Kid's Emerald Circus of Oz!

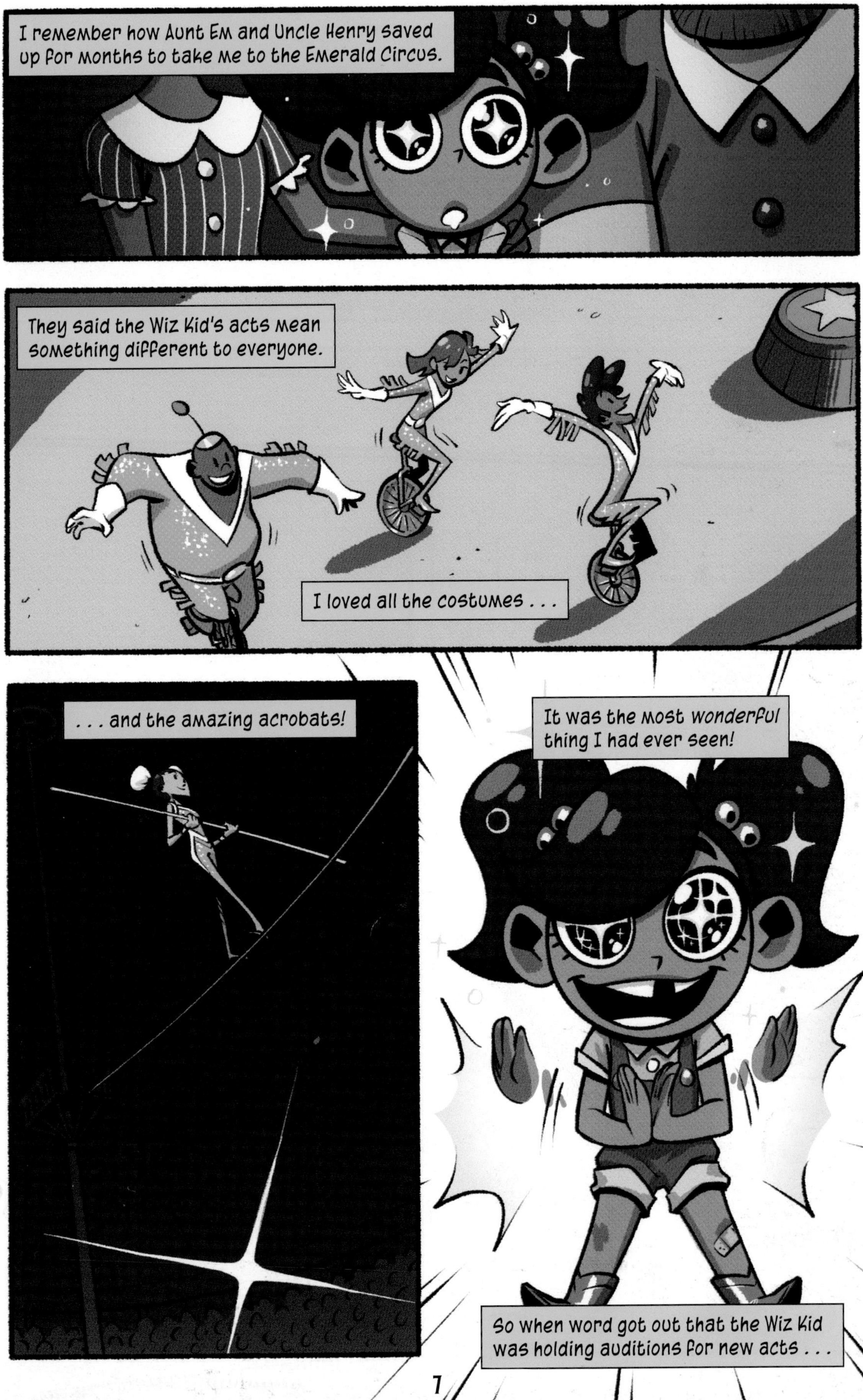
I remember how Aunt Em and Uncle Henry saved up for months to take me to the Emerald Circus.
They said the Wiz Kid's acts mean something different to everyone.
I loved all the costumes . . .
. . . and the amazing acrobats!
It was the most *wonderful* thing I had ever seen!
So when word got out that the Wiz Kid was holding auditions for new acts . . .

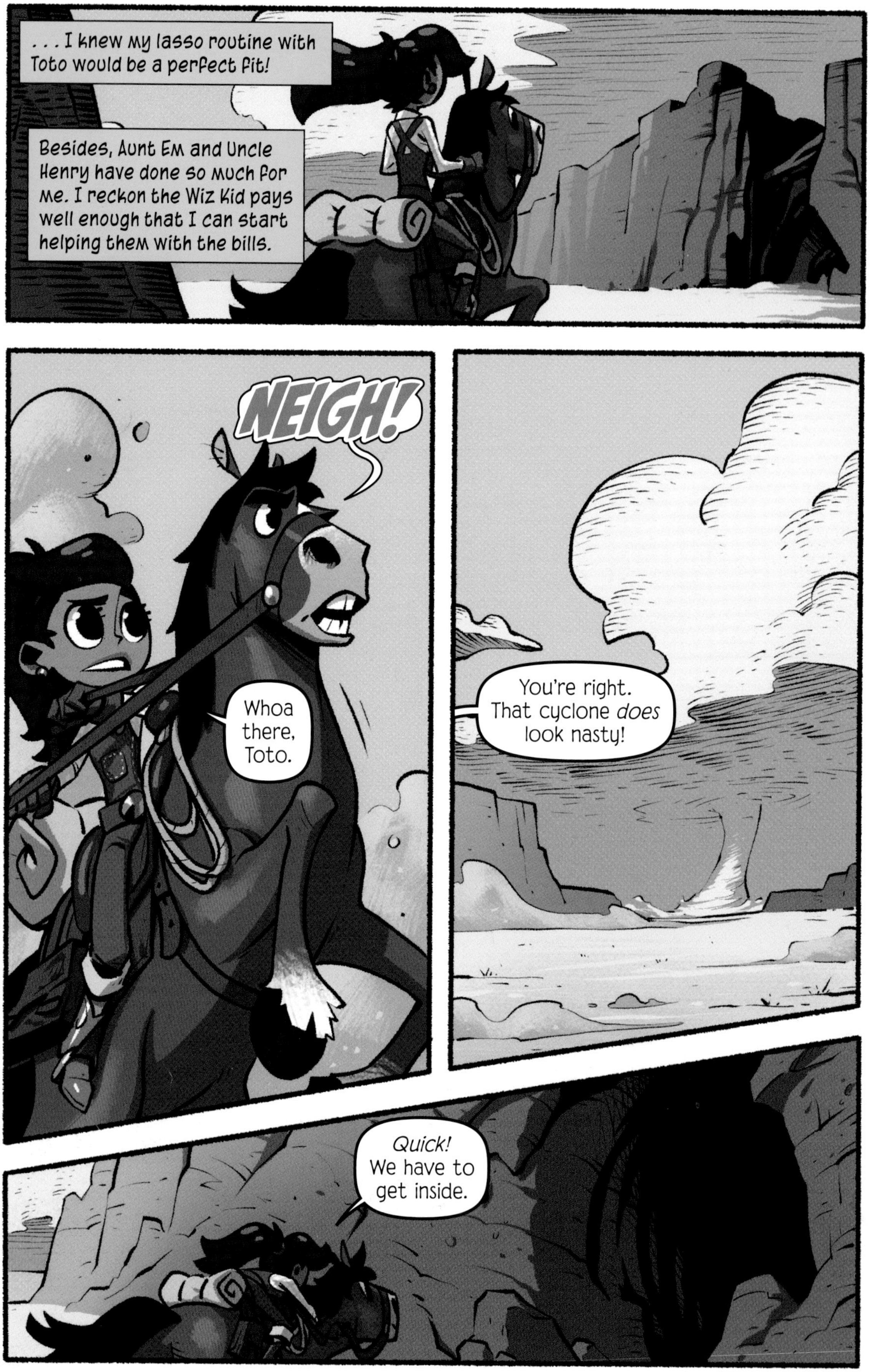
. . . I knew my lasso routine with Toto would be a perfect fit!
Besides, Aunt Em and Uncle Henry have done so much for me. I reckon the Wiz Kid pays well enough that I can start helping them with the bills.
NEIGH!
Whoa there, Toto.
You're right. That cyclone *does* look nasty!
Quick! We have to get inside.

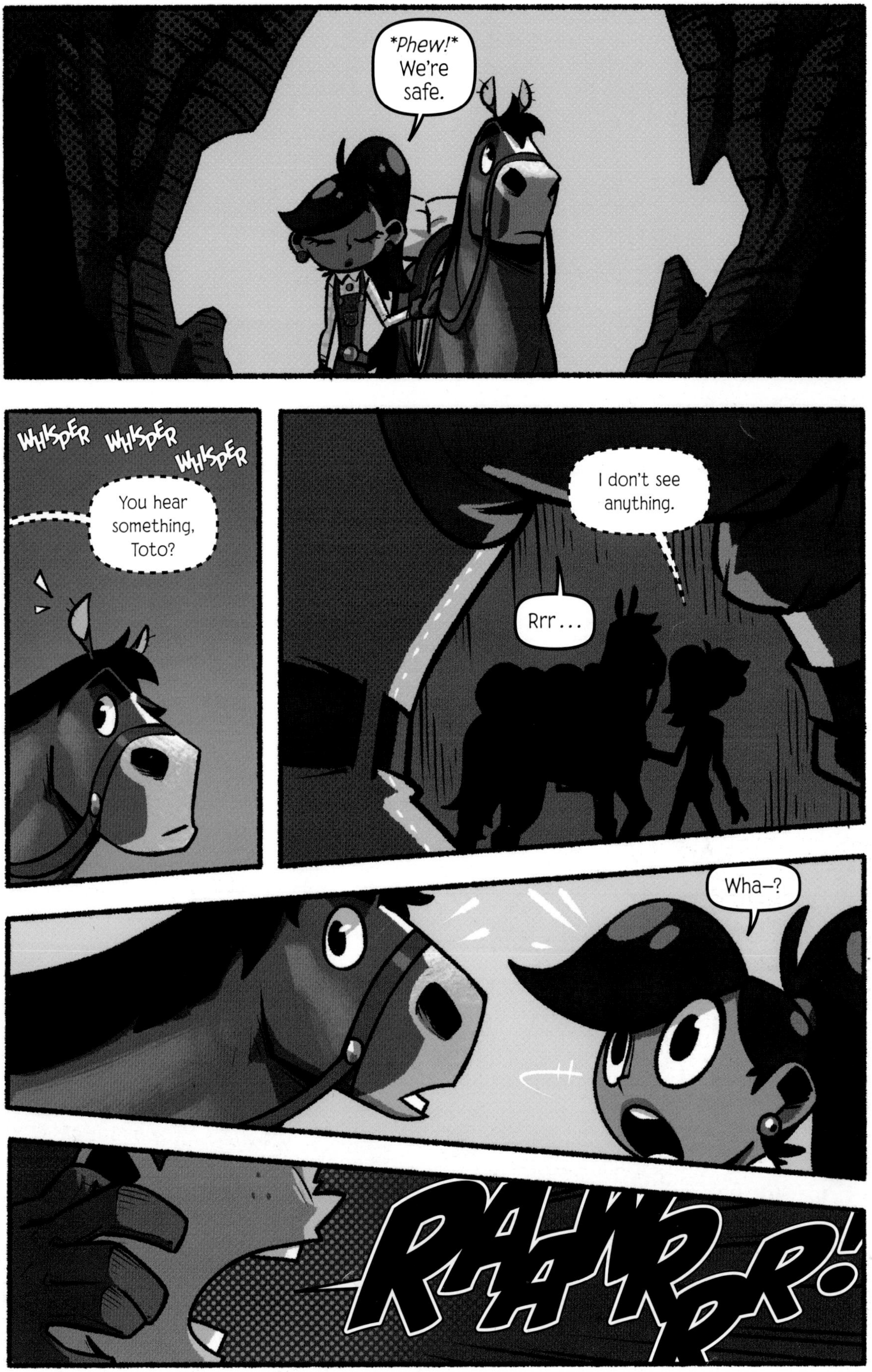
Phew! We're safe.
WHISPER WHISPER WHISPER
You hear something, Toto?
I don't see anything.
Rrr...
Wha–?
RAAWRRR!

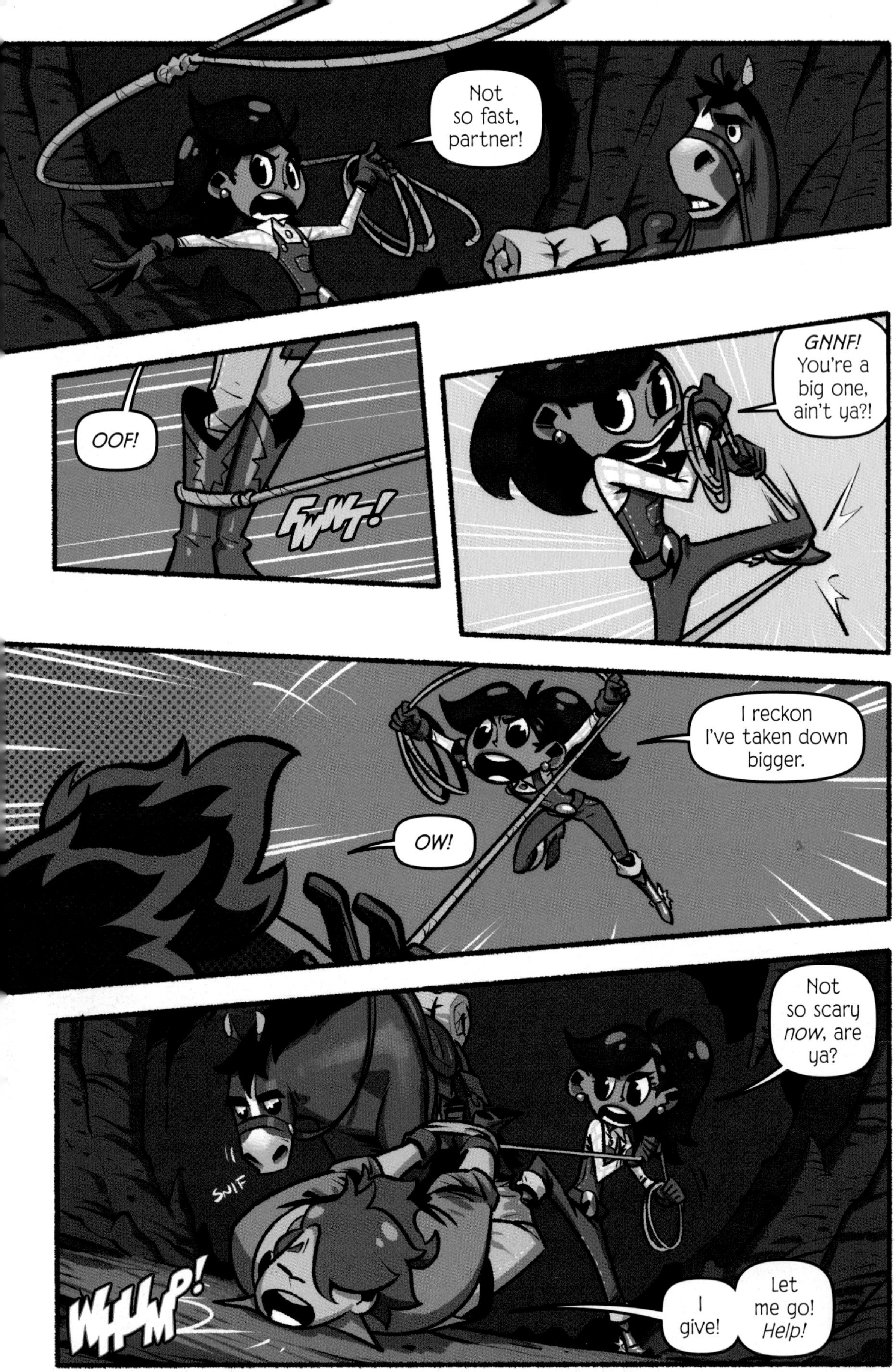

Not so fast, partner!
OOF!
FWWT!
GNNF! You're a big one, ain't ya?!
I reckon I've taken down bigger.
OW!
Not so scary now, are ya?
SNIF
WHUMP!
I give!
Let me go! Help!

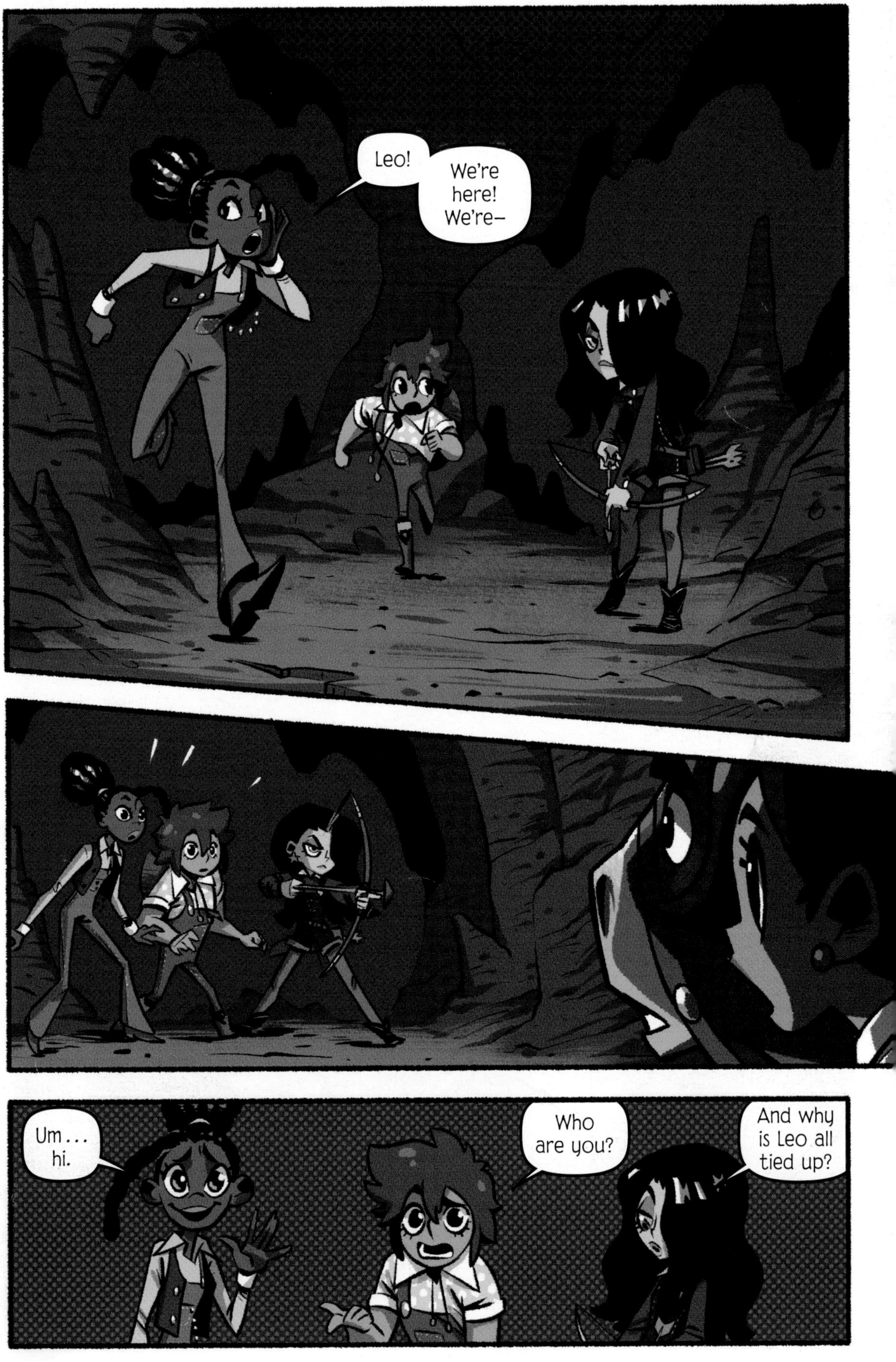
Leo!
We're here! We're–
Um... hi.
Who are you?
And why is Leo all tied up?

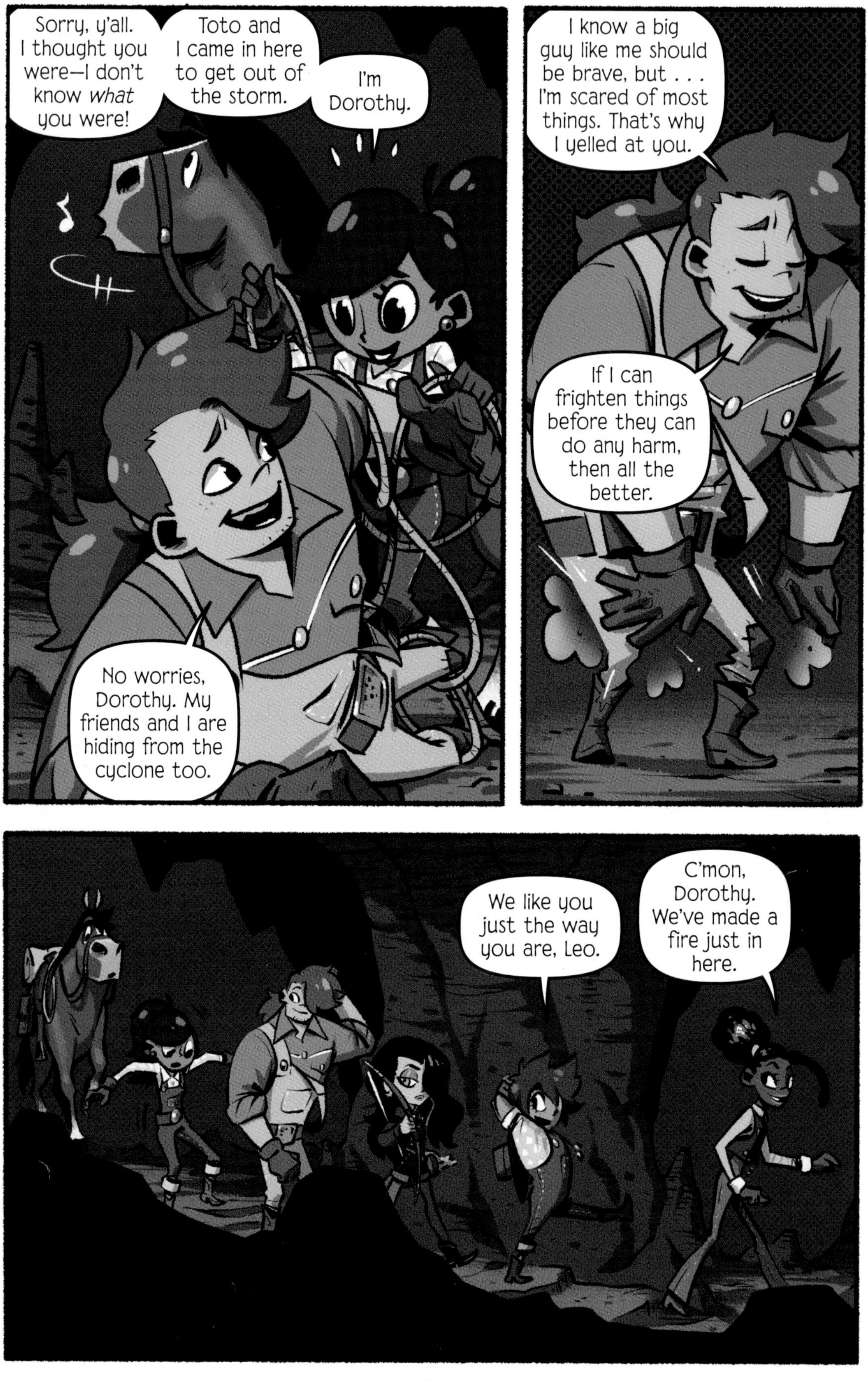
Sorry, y'all. I thought you were—I don't know *what* you were!
Toto and I came in here to get out of the storm.
I'm Dorothy.
No worries, Dorothy. My friends and I are hiding from the cyclone too.
I know a big guy like me should be brave, but . . . I'm scared of most things. That's why I yelled at you.
If I can frighten things before they can do any harm, then all the better.
We like you just the way you are, Leo.
C'mon, Dorothy. We've made a fire just in here.

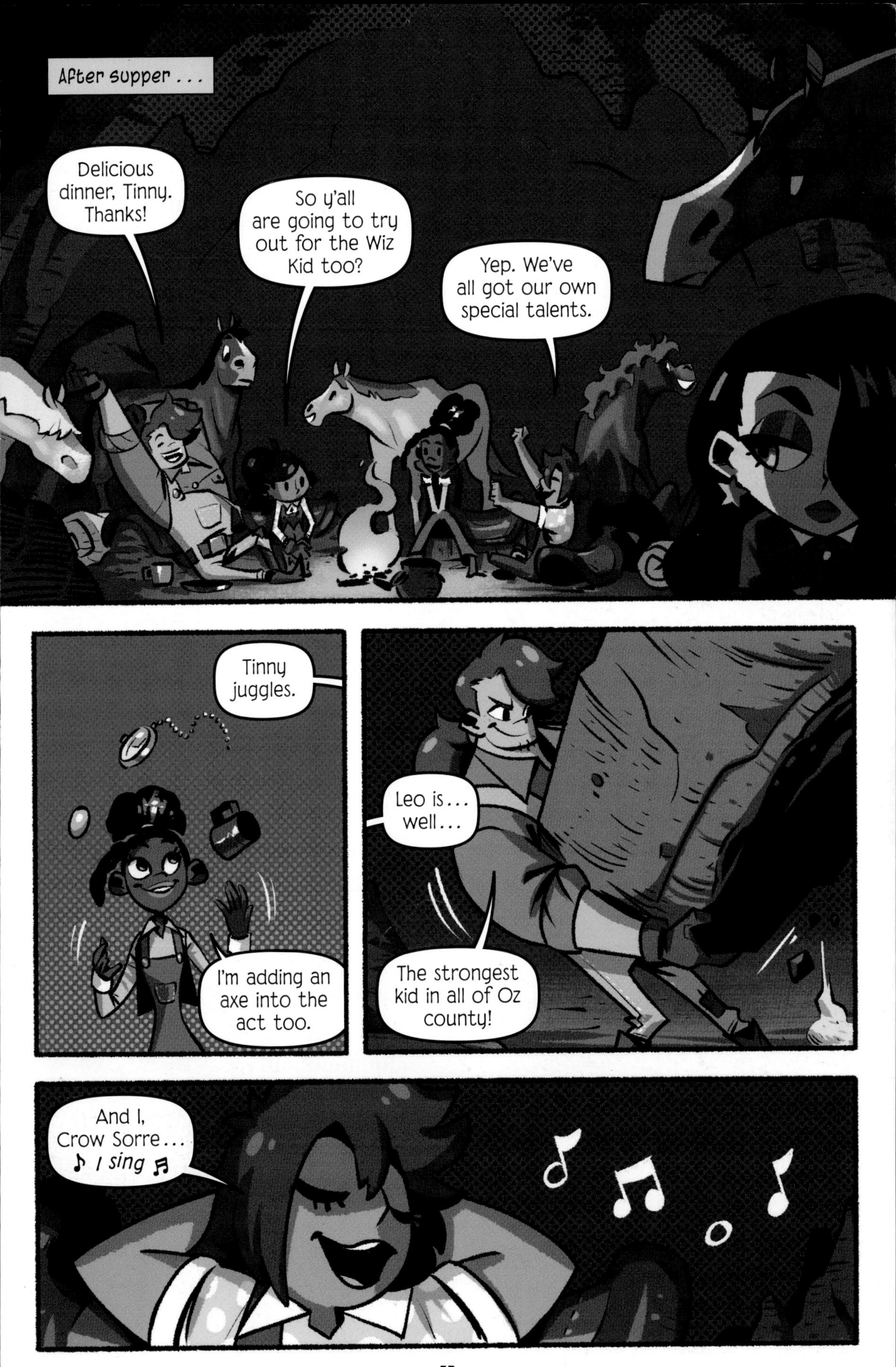
After supper . . .
Delicious dinner, Tinny. Thanks!
So y'all are going to try out for the Wiz Kid too?
Yep. We've all got our own special talents.
Tinny juggles.
I'm adding an axe into the act too.
Leo is... well...
The strongest kid in all of Oz county!
And I, Crow Sorre...
♪ I sing ♬

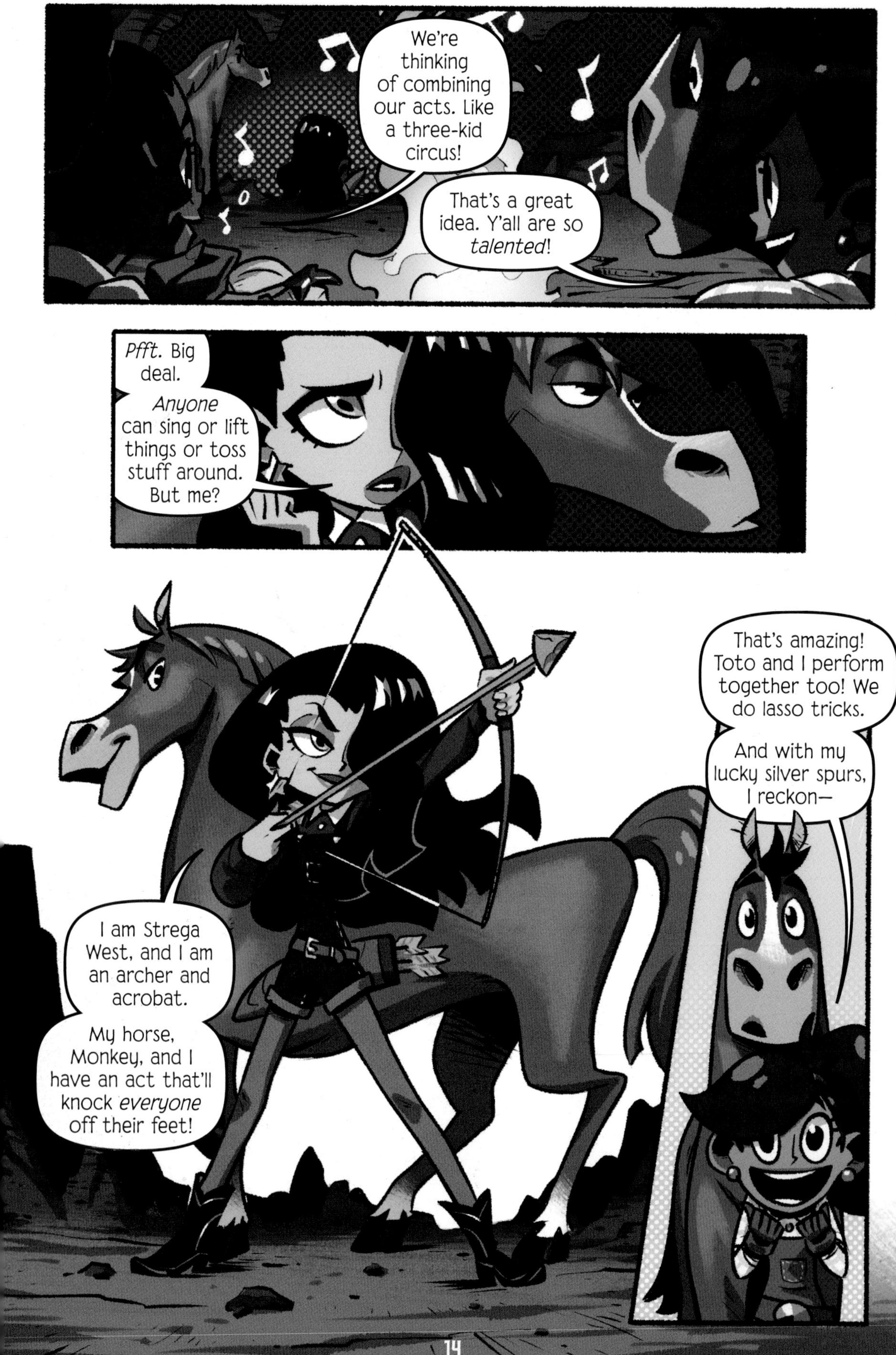
We're thinking of combining our acts. Like a three-kid circus!
That's a great idea. Y'all are so *talented*!
Pfft. Big deal.
Anyone can sing or lift things or toss stuff around. But me?
I am Strega West, and I am an archer and acrobat.
My horse, Monkey, and I have an act that'll knock *everyone* off their feet!
That's amazing! Toto and I perform together too! We do lasso tricks.
And with my lucky silver spurs, I reckon—

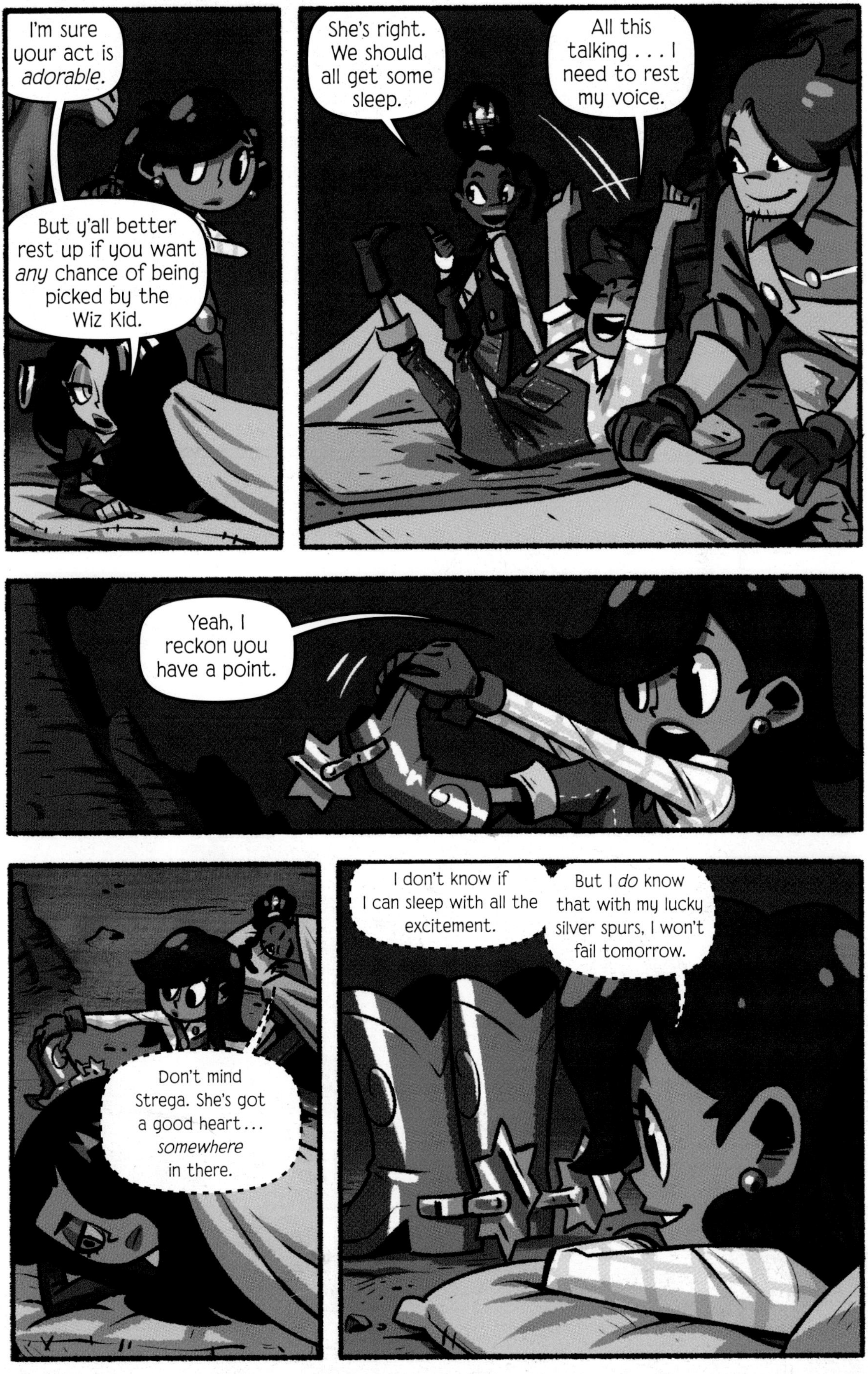
I'm sure your act is *adorable*.
But y'all better rest up if you want *any* chance of being picked by the Wiz Kid.
She's right. We should all get some sleep.
All this talking . . . I need to rest my voice.
Yeah, I reckon you have a point.
Don't mind Strega. She's got a good heart . . . *somewhere* in there.
I don't know if I can sleep with all the excitement.
But I *do* know that with my lucky silver spurs, I won't fail tomorrow.

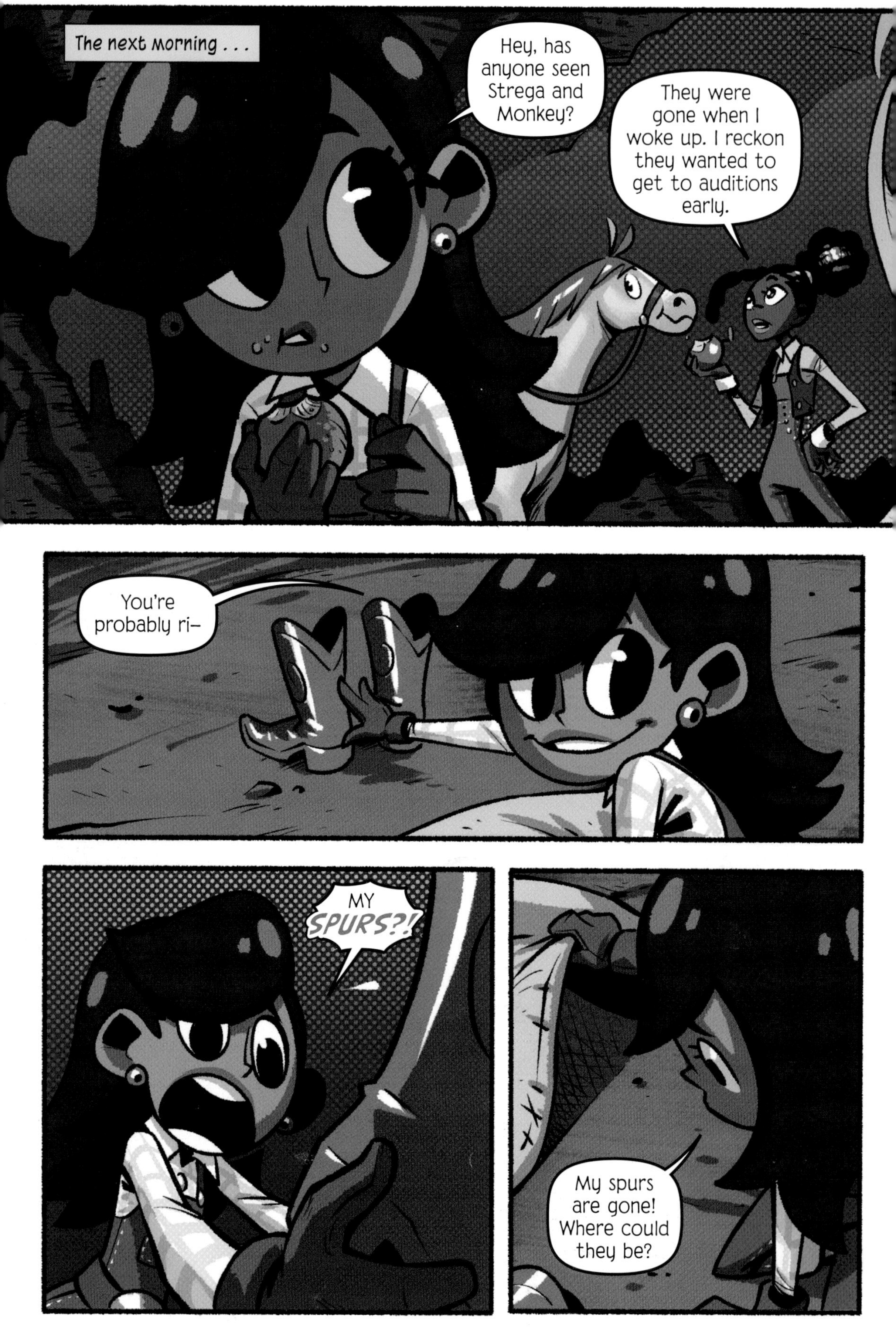

The next morning . . .
Hey, has anyone seen Strega and Monkey?
They were gone when I woke up. I reckon they wanted to get to auditions early.
You're probably ri–
MY SPURS?!
My spurs are gone! Where could they be?

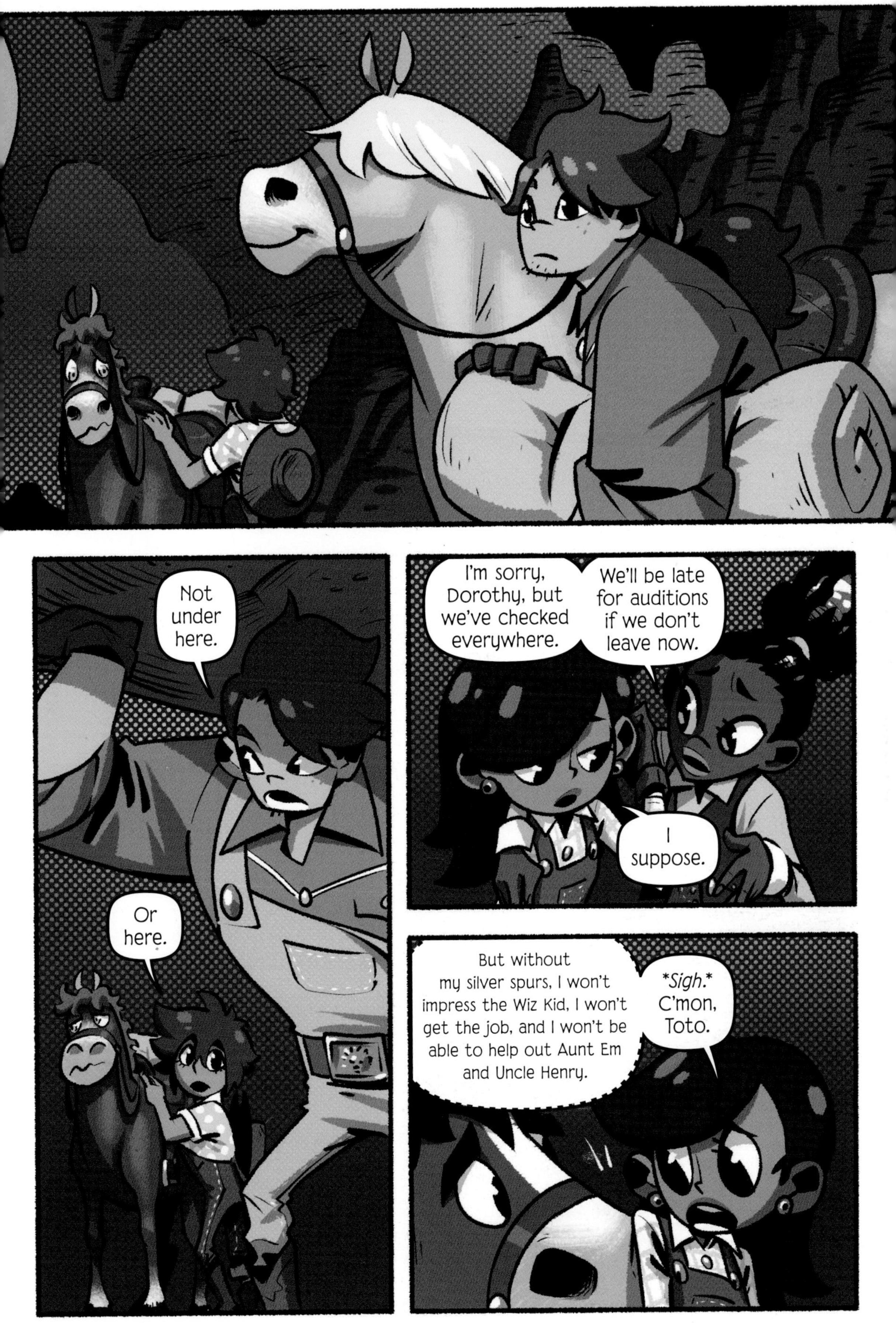
Not under here.
Or here.
I'm sorry, Dorothy, but we've checked everywhere.
We'll be late for auditions if we don't leave now.
I suppose.
But without my silver spurs, I won't impress the Wiz Kid, I won't get the job, and I won't be able to help out Aunt Em and Uncle Henry.
Sigh. C'mon, Toto.

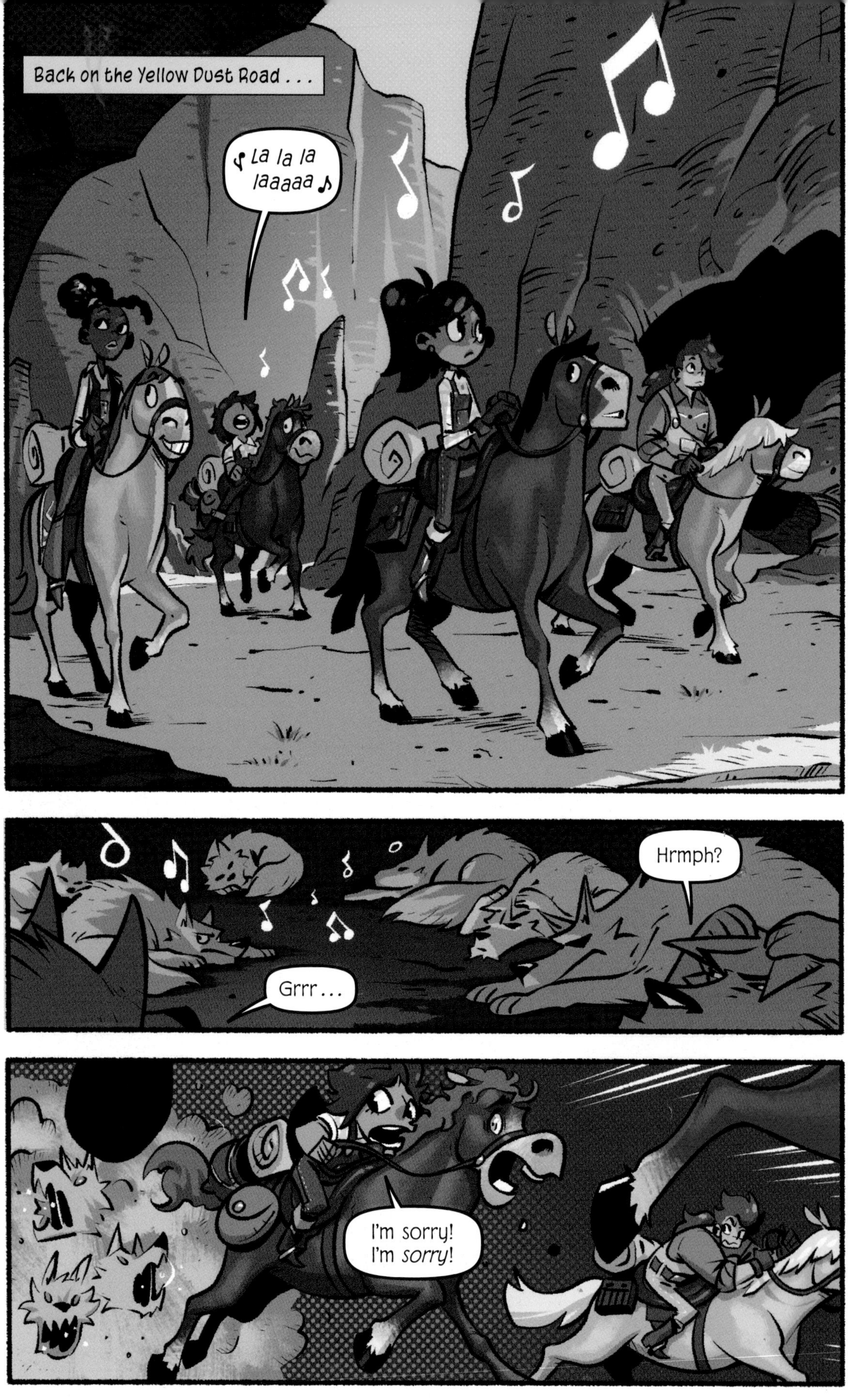

Back on the Yellow Dust Road . . .
La la la laaaaa
Hrmph?
Grrr . . .
I'm sorry! I'm *sorry*!

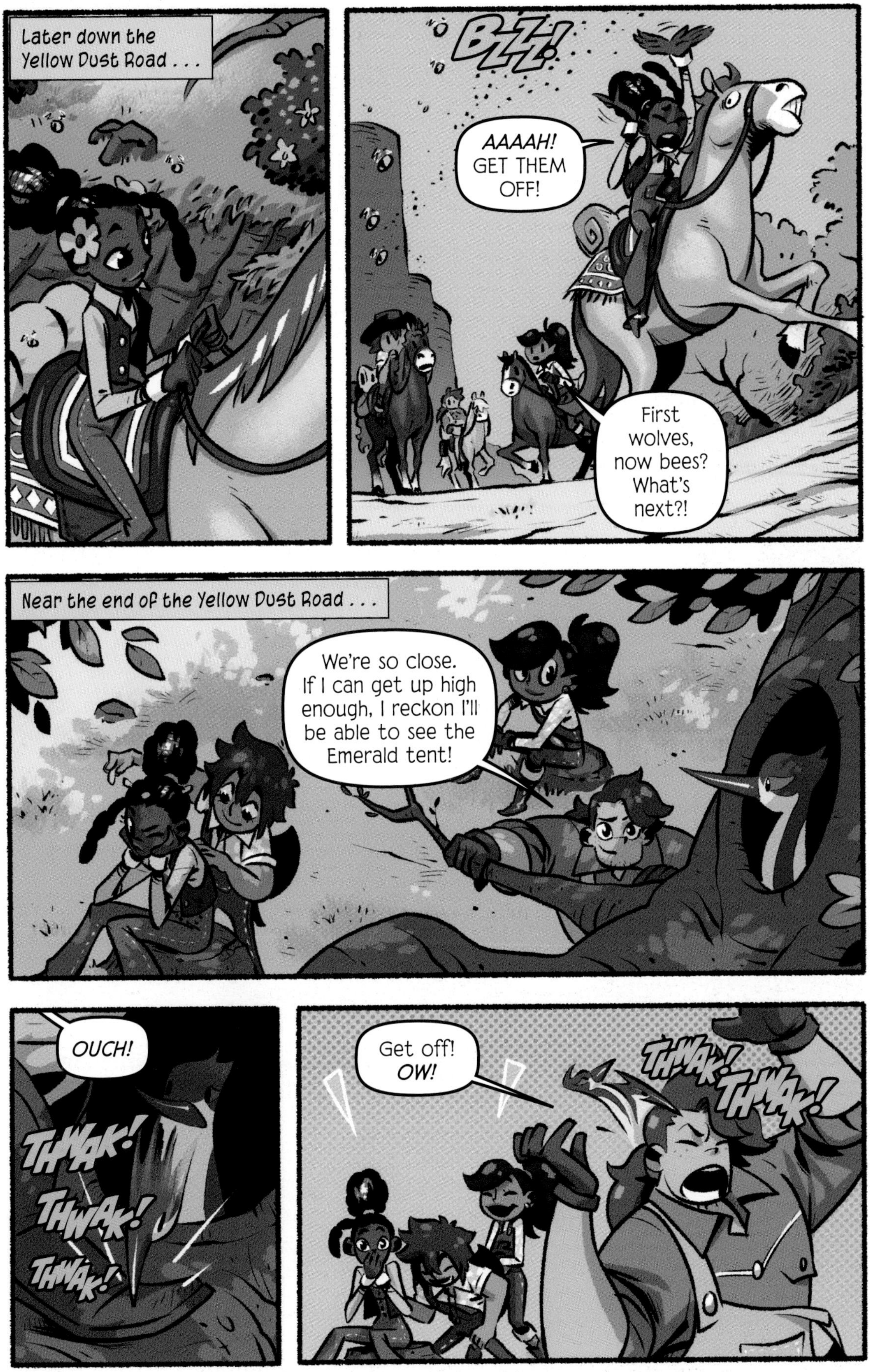

Later down the Yellow Dust Road . . .
BZZZ!
AAAAH! GET THEM OFF!
First wolves, now bees? What's next?!
Near the end of the Yellow Dust Road . . .
We're so close. If I can get up high enough, I reckon I'll be able to see the Emerald tent!
OUCH!
THWAK!
THWAK!
THWAK!
Get off! OW!
THWAK! THWAK!

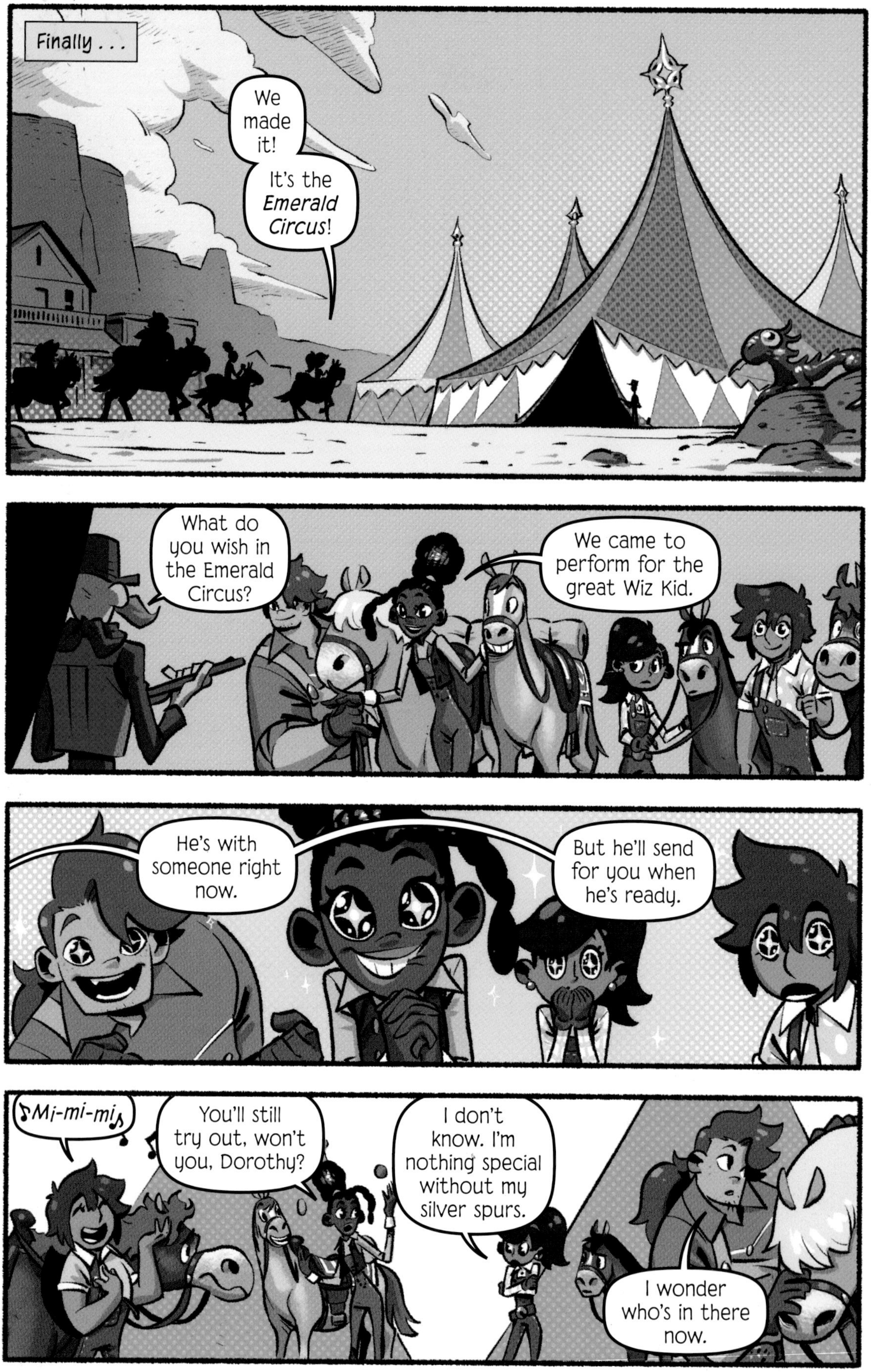
Finally . . .
We made it!
It's the *Emerald Circus*!
What do you wish in the Emerald Circus?
We came to perform for the great Wiz Kid.
He's with someone right now.
But he'll send for you when he's ready.
Mi-mi-mi
You'll still try out, won't you, Dorothy?
I don't know. I'm nothing special without my silver spurs.
I wonder who's in there now.

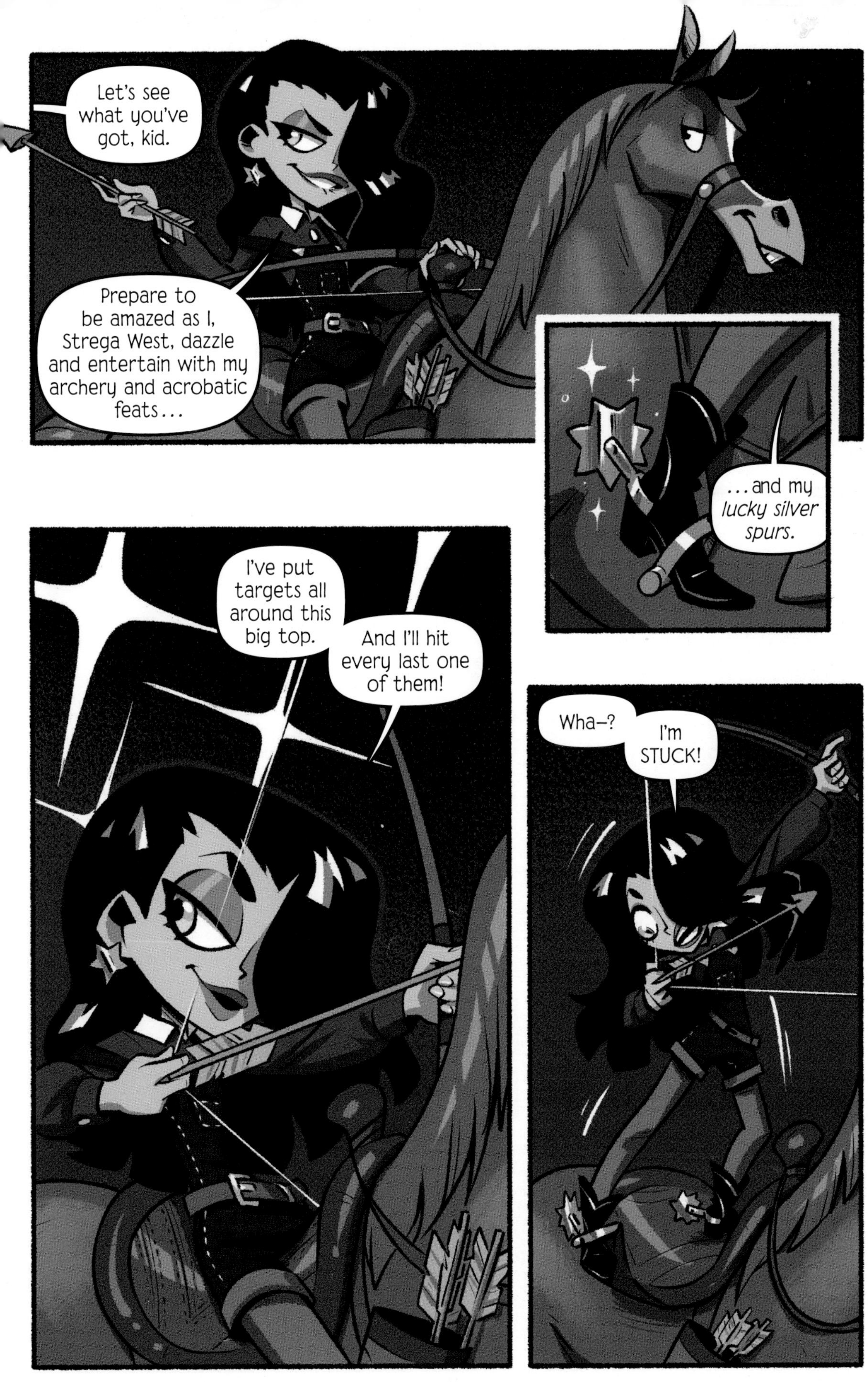
Let's see what you've got, kid.
Prepare to be amazed as I, Strega West, dazzle and entertain with my archery and acrobatic feats...
...and my *lucky silver spurs.*
I've put targets all around this big top.
And I'll hit every last one of them!
Wha–?
I'm STUCK!

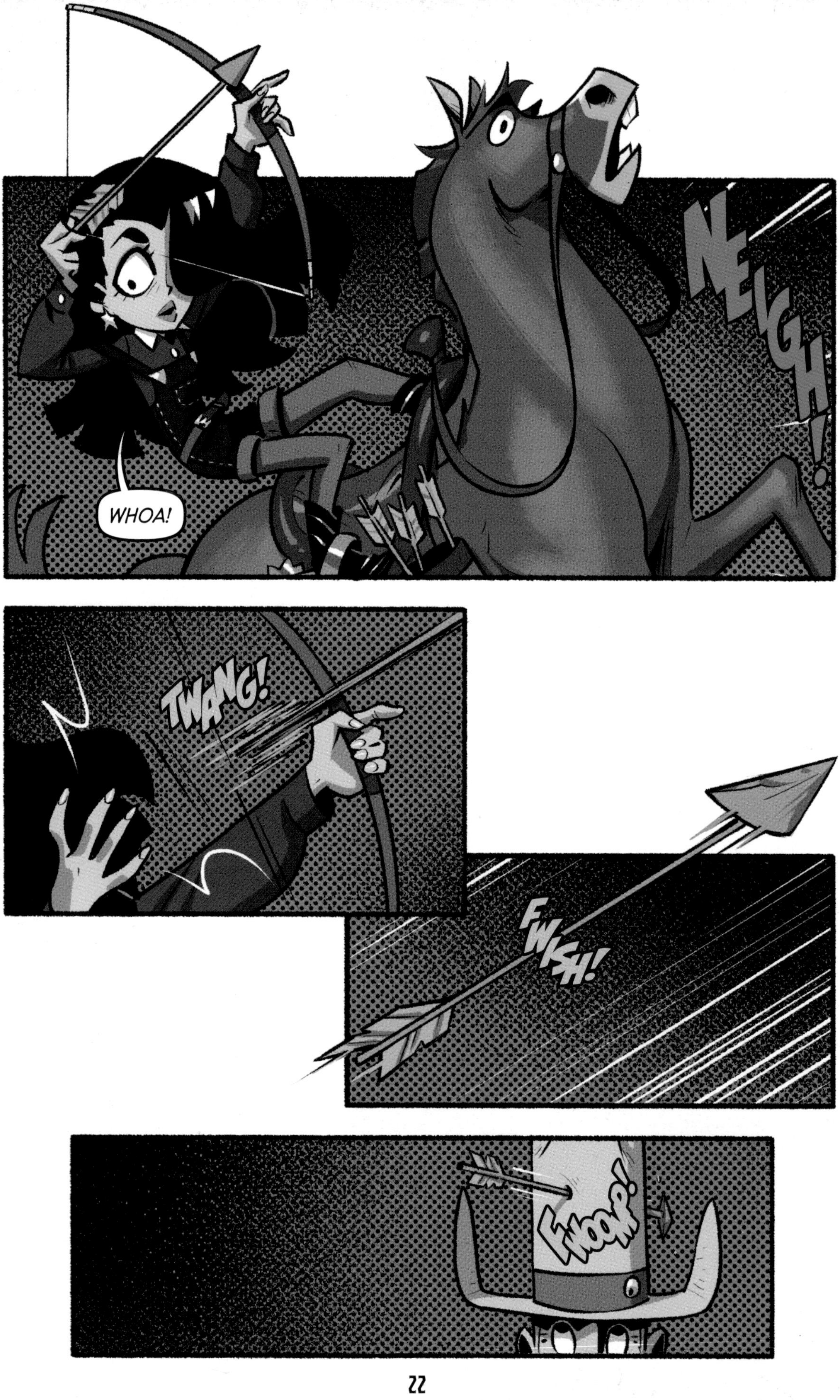
WHOA!
NEIGH!
TWANG!
FWISH!
FWOOP!

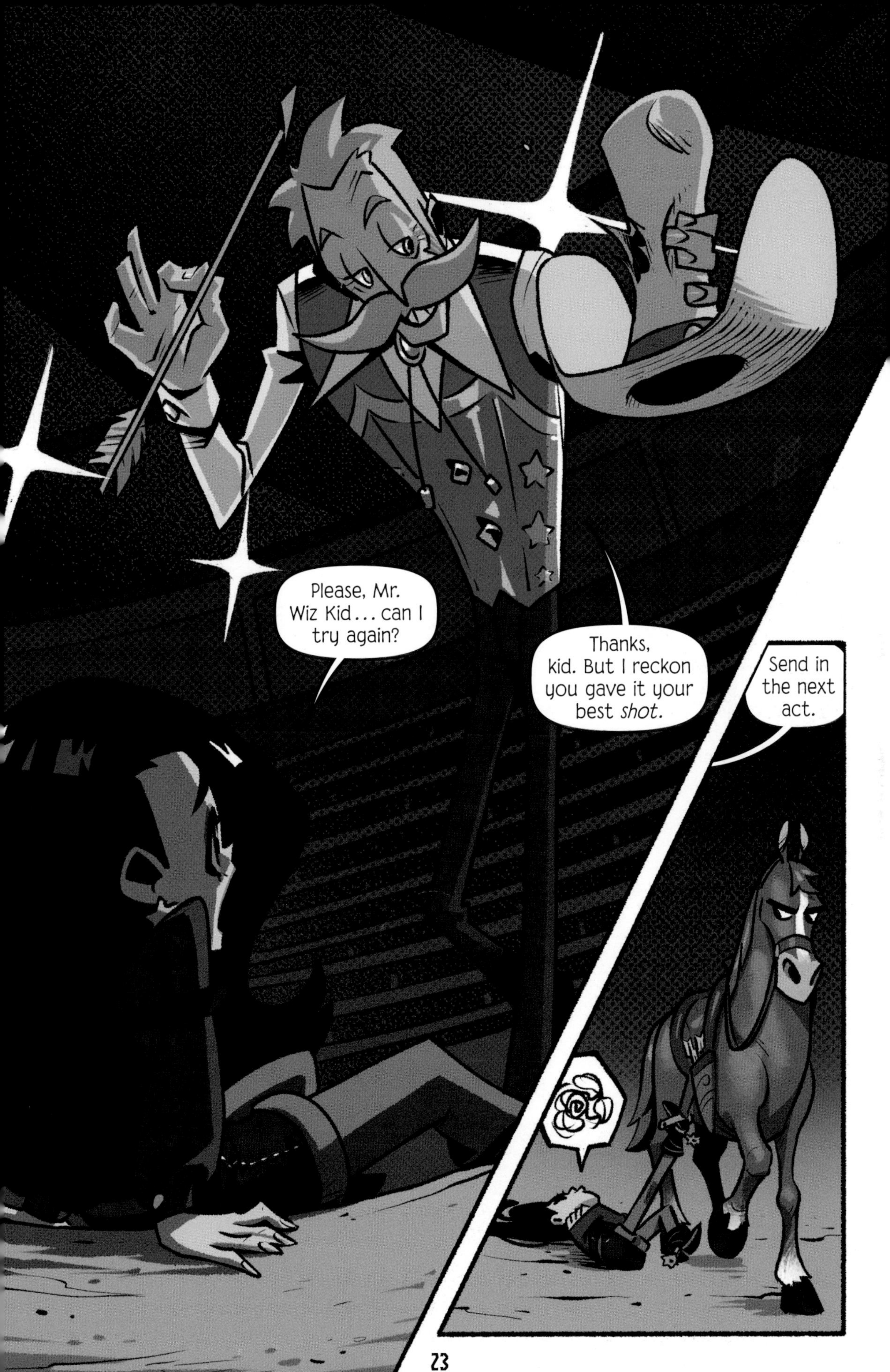
Please, Mr. Wiz Kid... can I try again?
Thanks, kid. But I reckon you gave it your best *shot*.
Send in the next act.

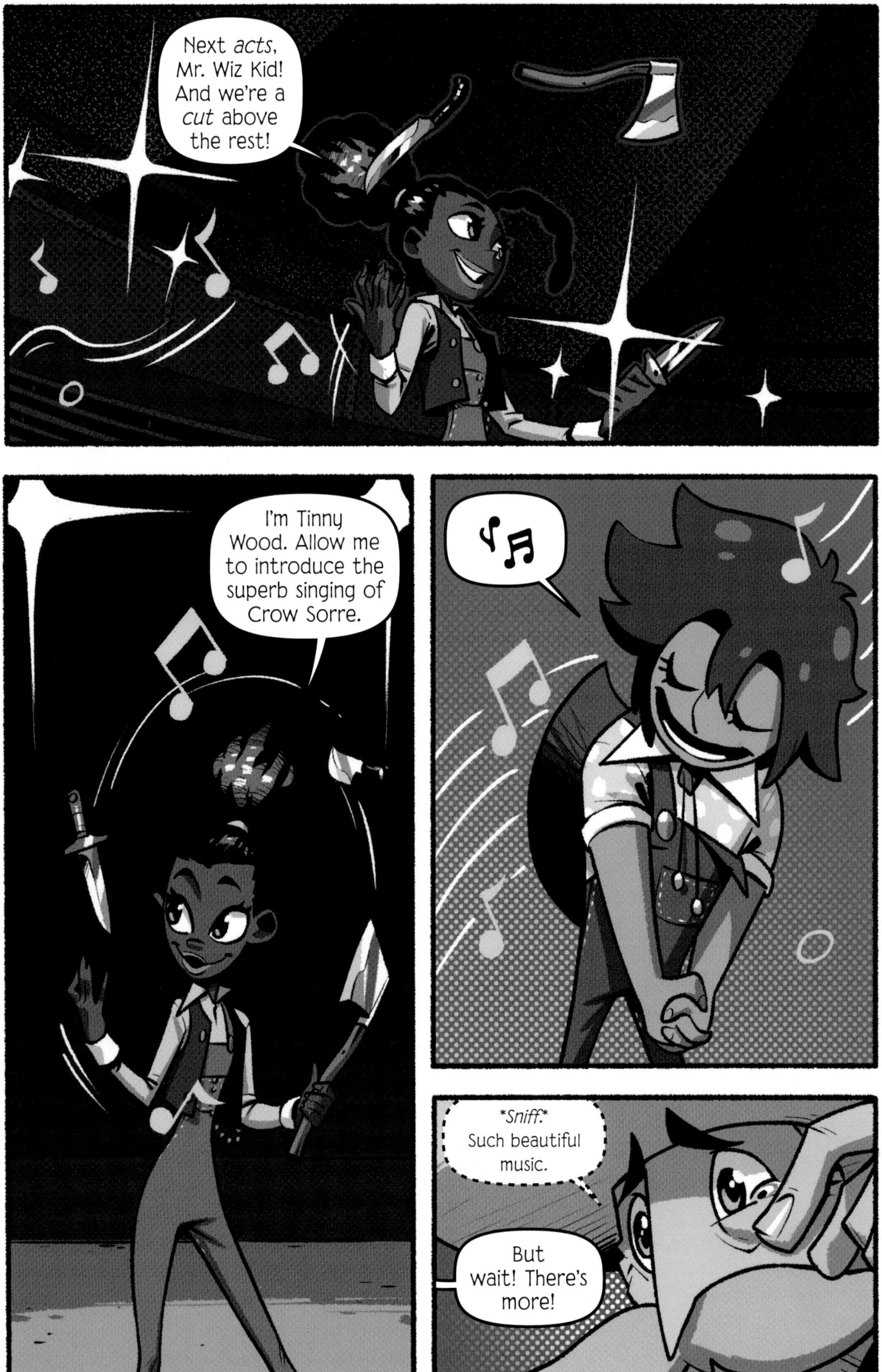
Next *acts*, Mr. Wiz Kid! And we're a *cut* above the rest!
I'm Tinny Wood. Allow me to introduce the superb singing of Crow Sorre.
Sniff. Such beautiful music.
But wait! There's more!

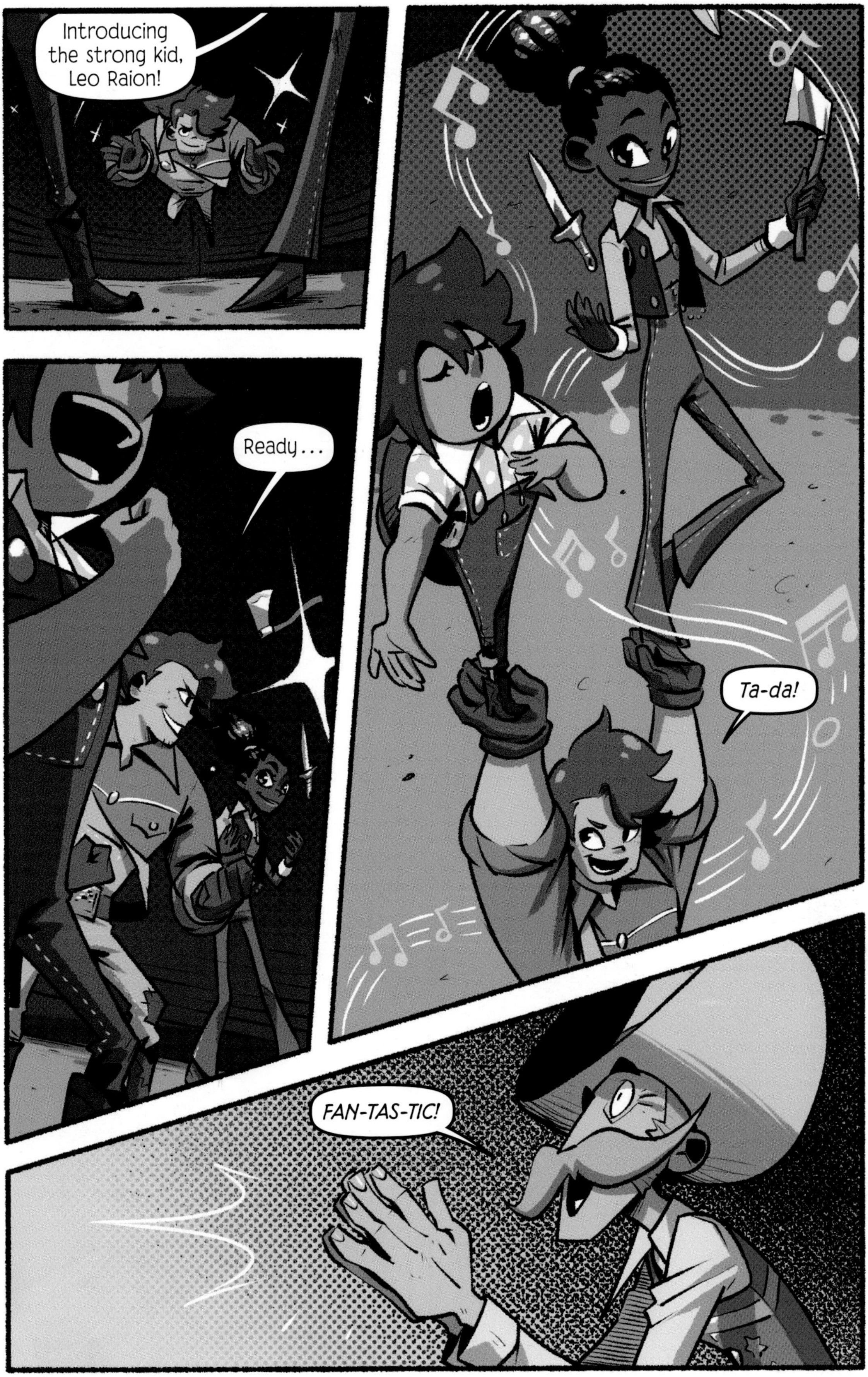
Introducing the strong kid, Leo Raion!
Ready...
Ta-da!
FAN-TAS-TIC!

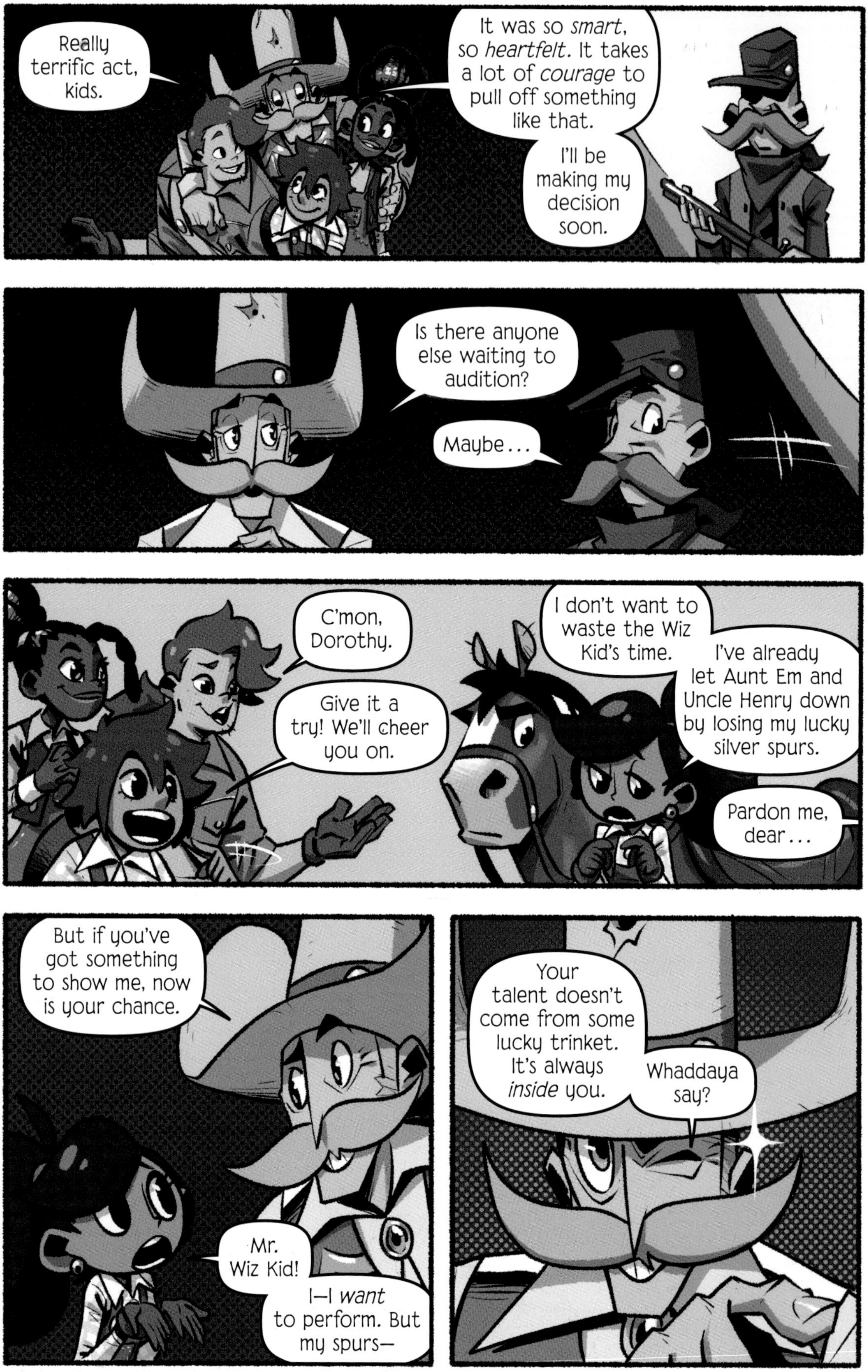
Really terrific act, kids.
It was so *smart*, so *heartfelt*. It takes a lot of *courage* to pull off something like that.
I'll be making my decision soon.
Is there anyone else waiting to audition?
Maybe...
C'mon, Dorothy.
Give it a try! We'll cheer you on.
I don't want to waste the Wiz Kid's time.
I've already let Aunt Em and Uncle Henry down by losing my lucky silver spurs.
Pardon me, dear...
But if you've got something to show me, now is your chance.
Mr. Wiz Kid!
I—I *want* to perform. But my spurs—
Your talent doesn't come from some lucky trinket. It's always *inside* you.
Whaddaya say?

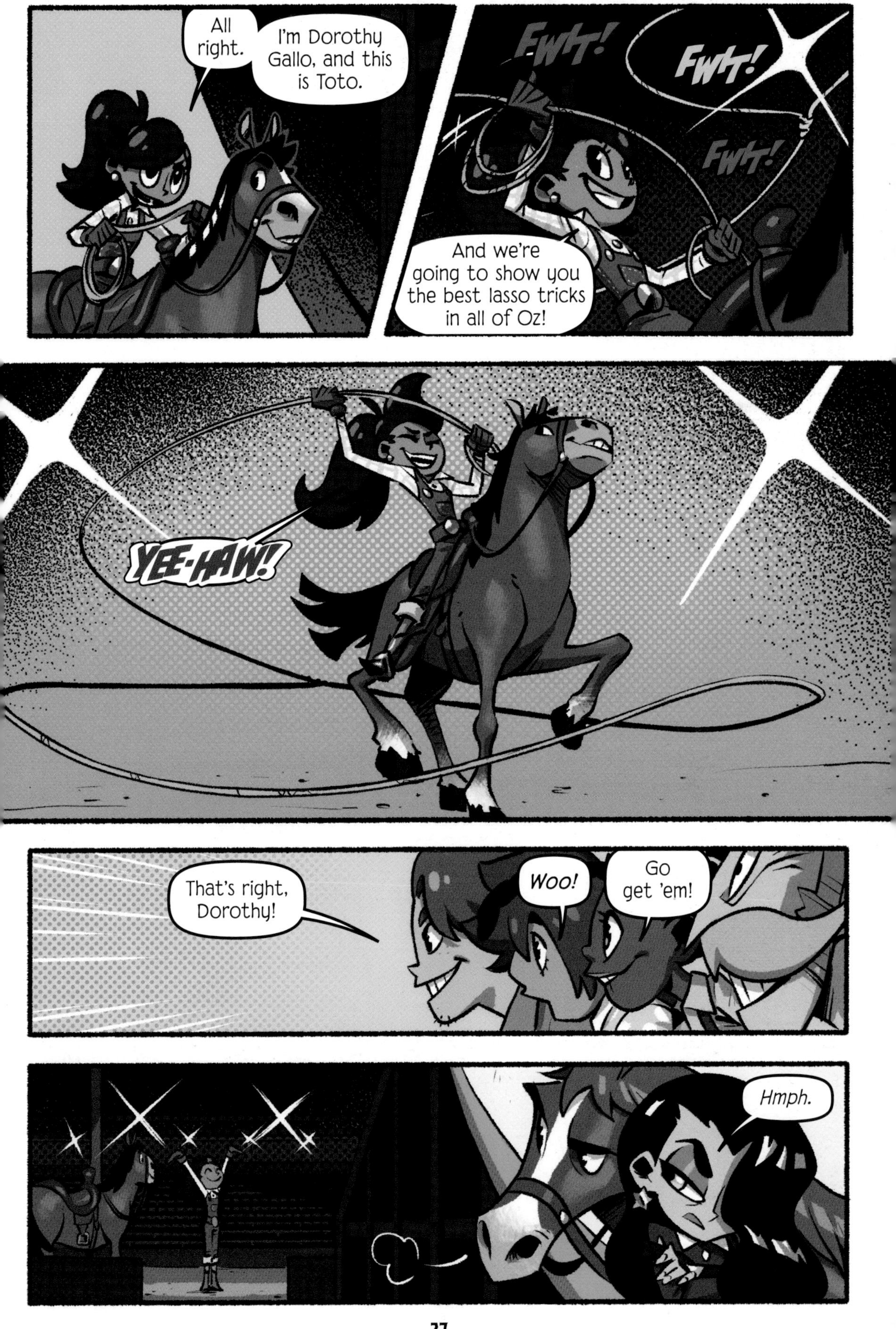
All right.
I'm Dorothy Gallo, and this is Toto.
FWIT!
FWIT!
FWIT!
And we're going to show you the best lasso tricks in all of Oz!
YEE-HAW!
That's right, Dorothy!
Woo!
Go get 'em!
Hmph.

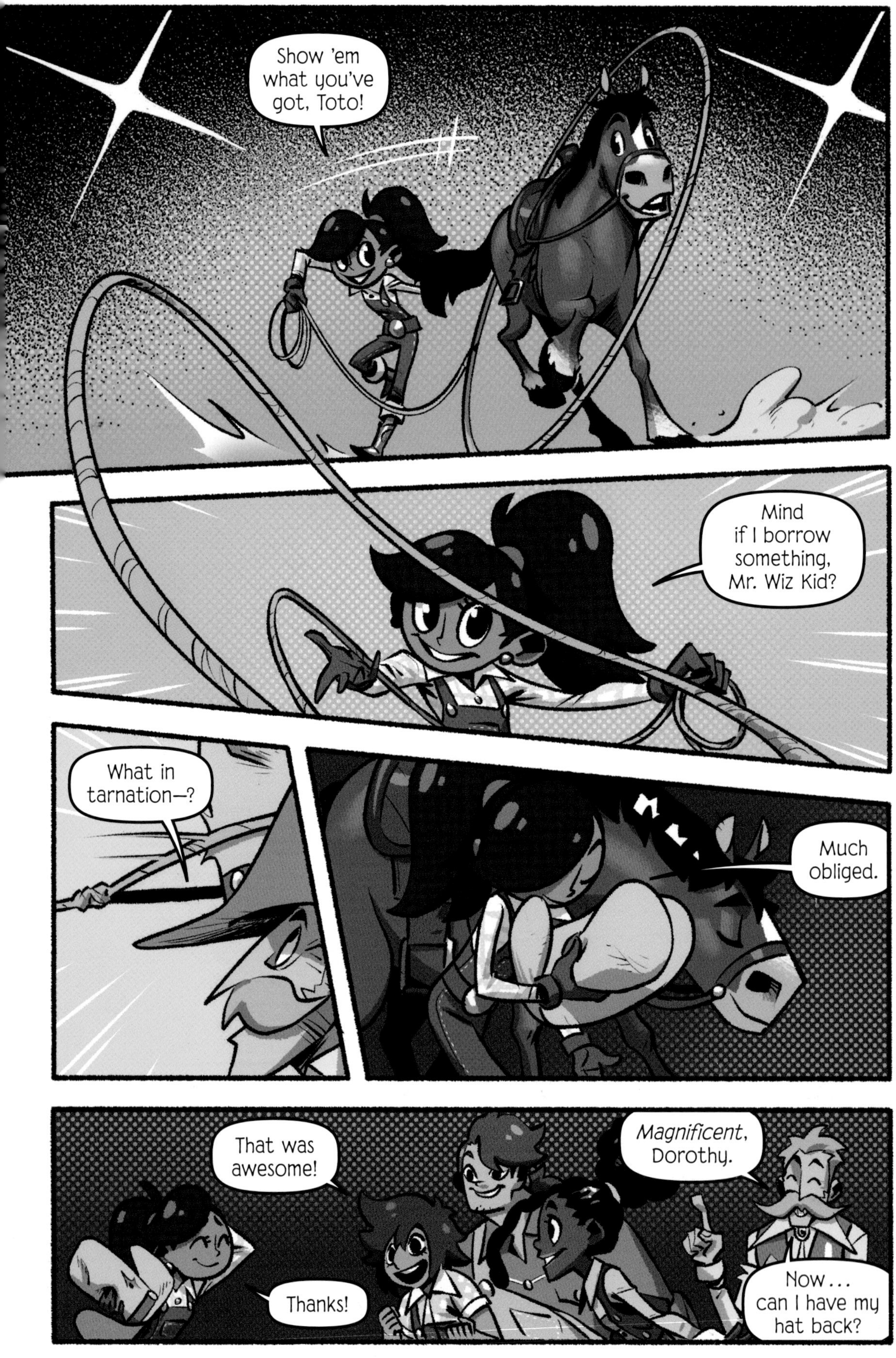
Show 'em what you've got, Toto!
Mind if I borrow something, Mr. Wiz Kid?
What in tarnation—?
Much obliged.
That was awesome!
Magnificent, Dorothy.
Thanks!
Now... can I have my hat back?

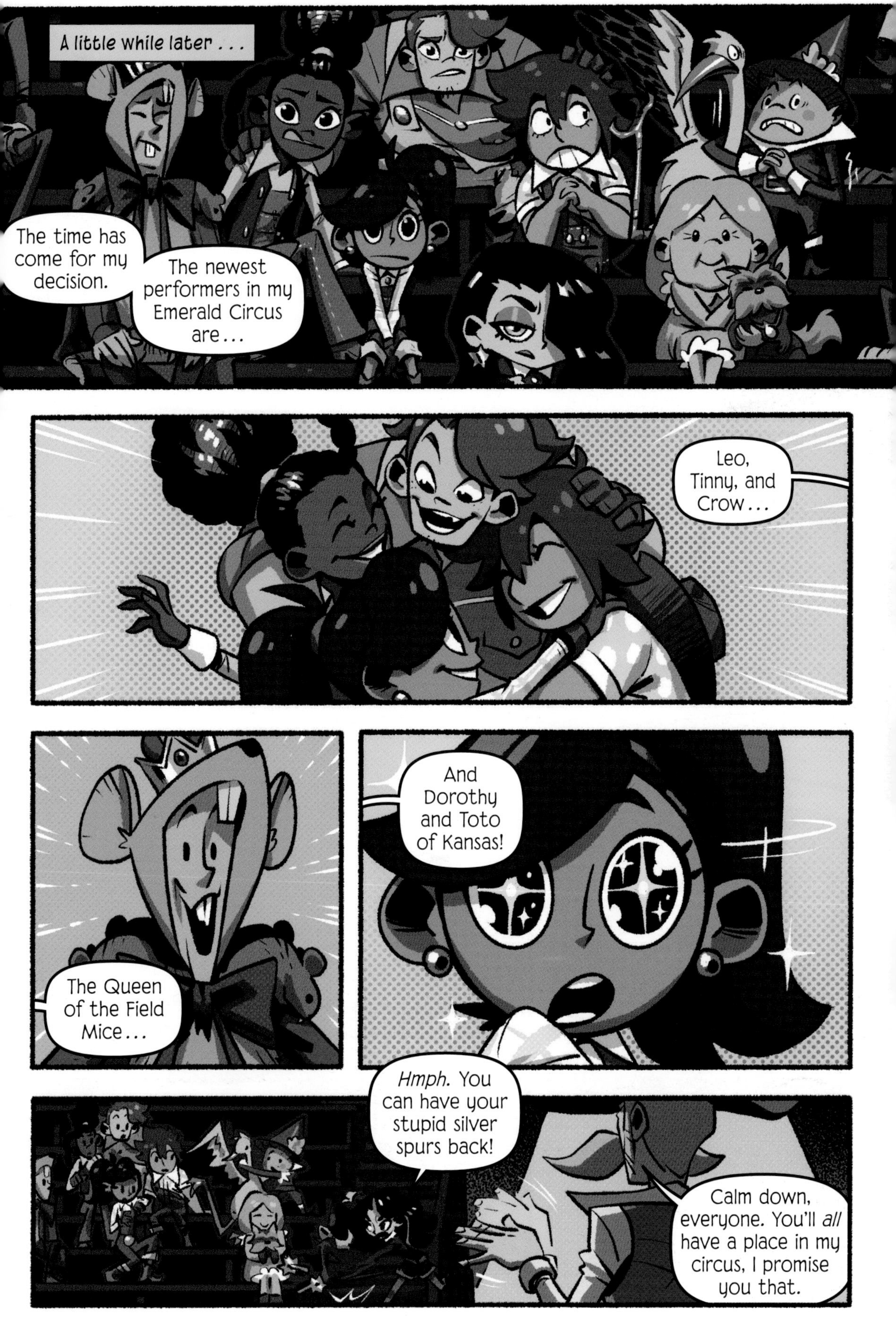
A little while later . . .
The time has come for my decision.
The newest performers in my Emerald Circus are...
Leo, Tinny, and Crow...
The Queen of the Field Mice...
And Dorothy and Toto of Kansas!
Hmph. You can have your stupid silver spurs back!
Calm down, everyone. You'll *all* have a place in my circus, I promise you that.

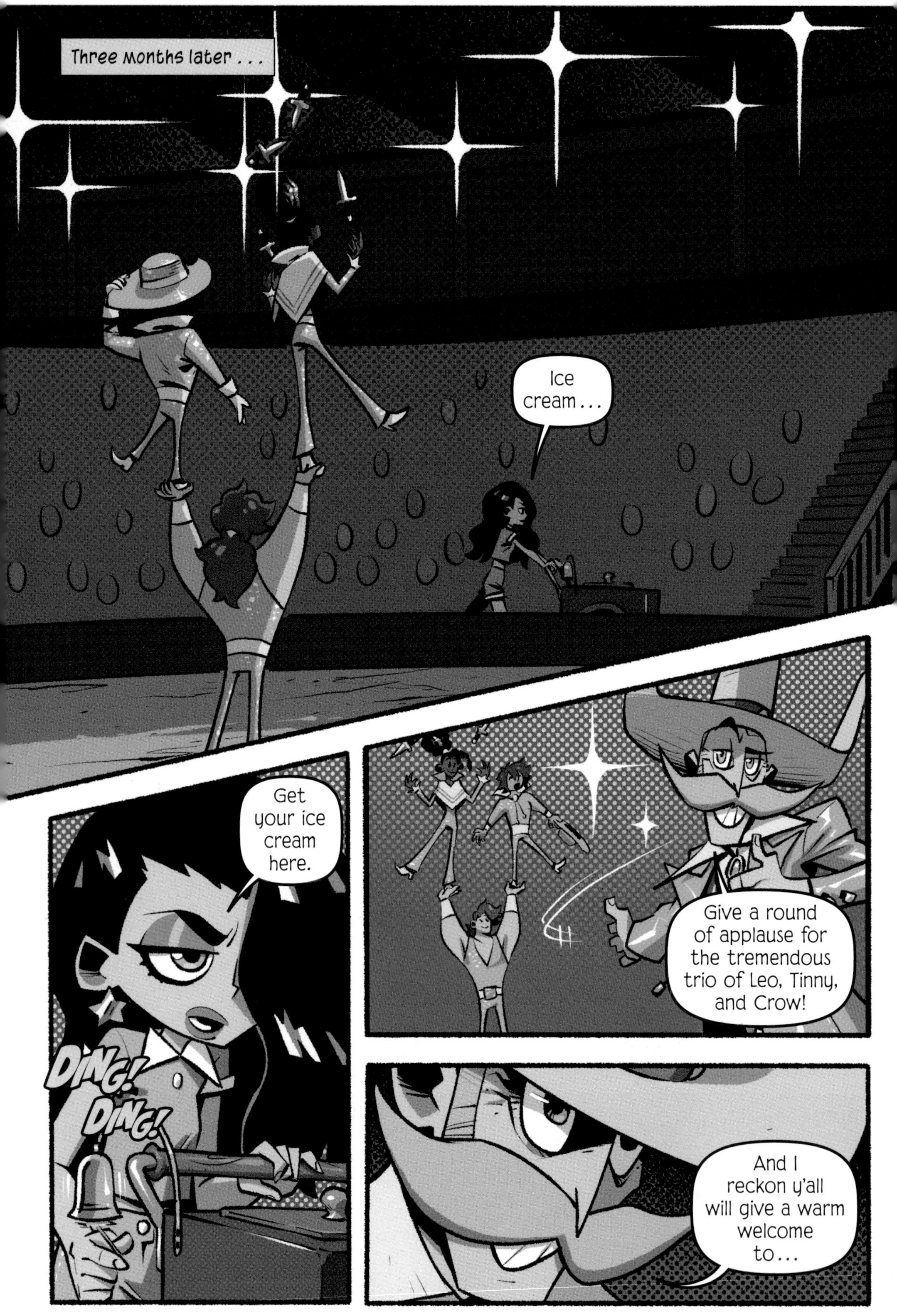
Three months later . . .
Ice cream . . .
Get your ice cream here.
DING! DING!
Give a round of applause for the tremendous trio of Leo, Tinny, and Crow!
And I reckon y'all will give a warm welcome to . . .

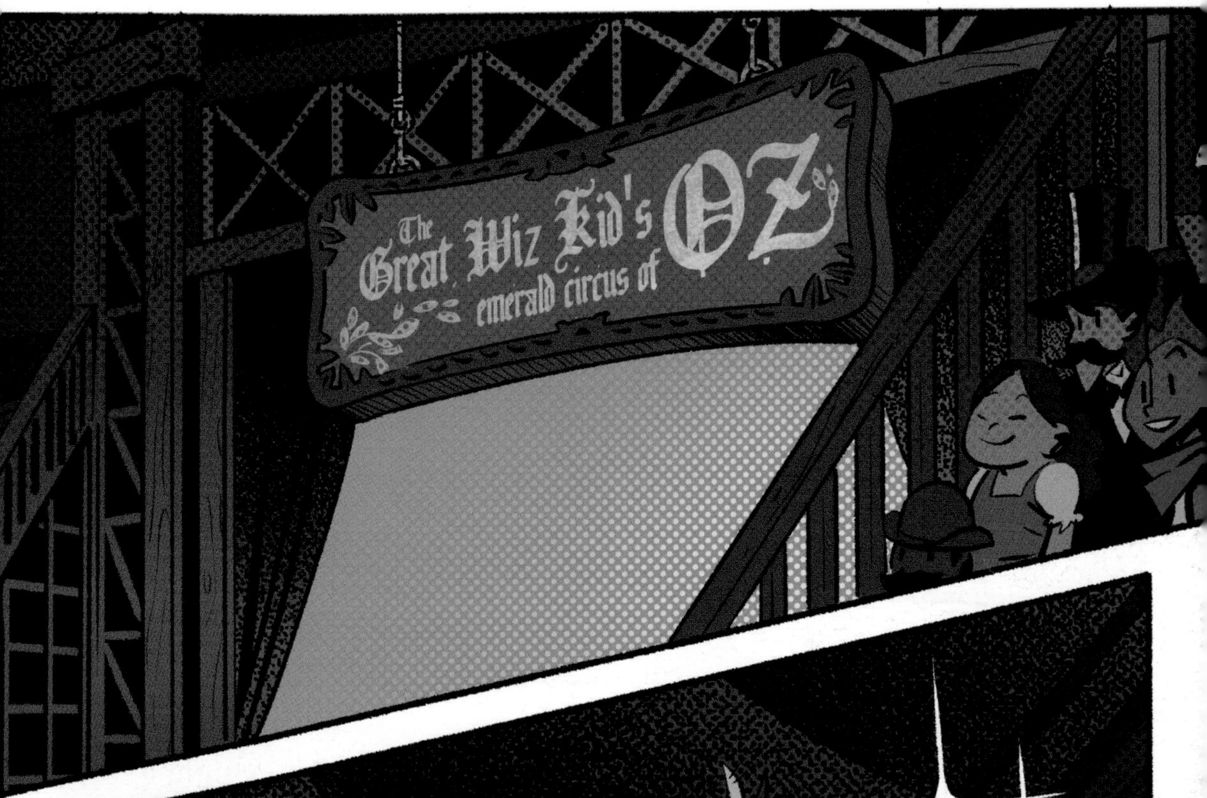
The Great Wiz Kid's emerald circus of OZ

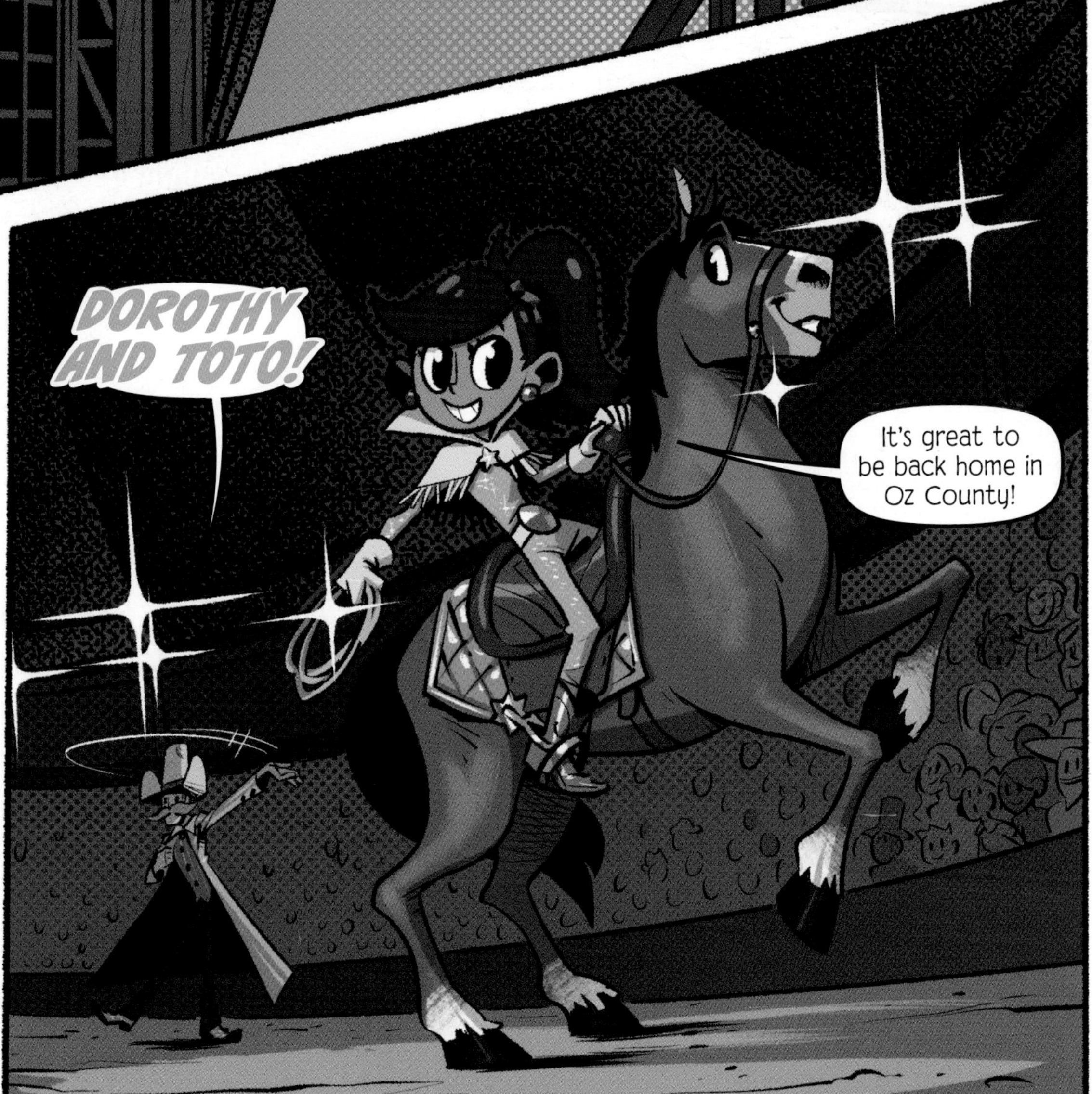
DOROTHY AND TOTO!
It's great to be back home in Oz County!

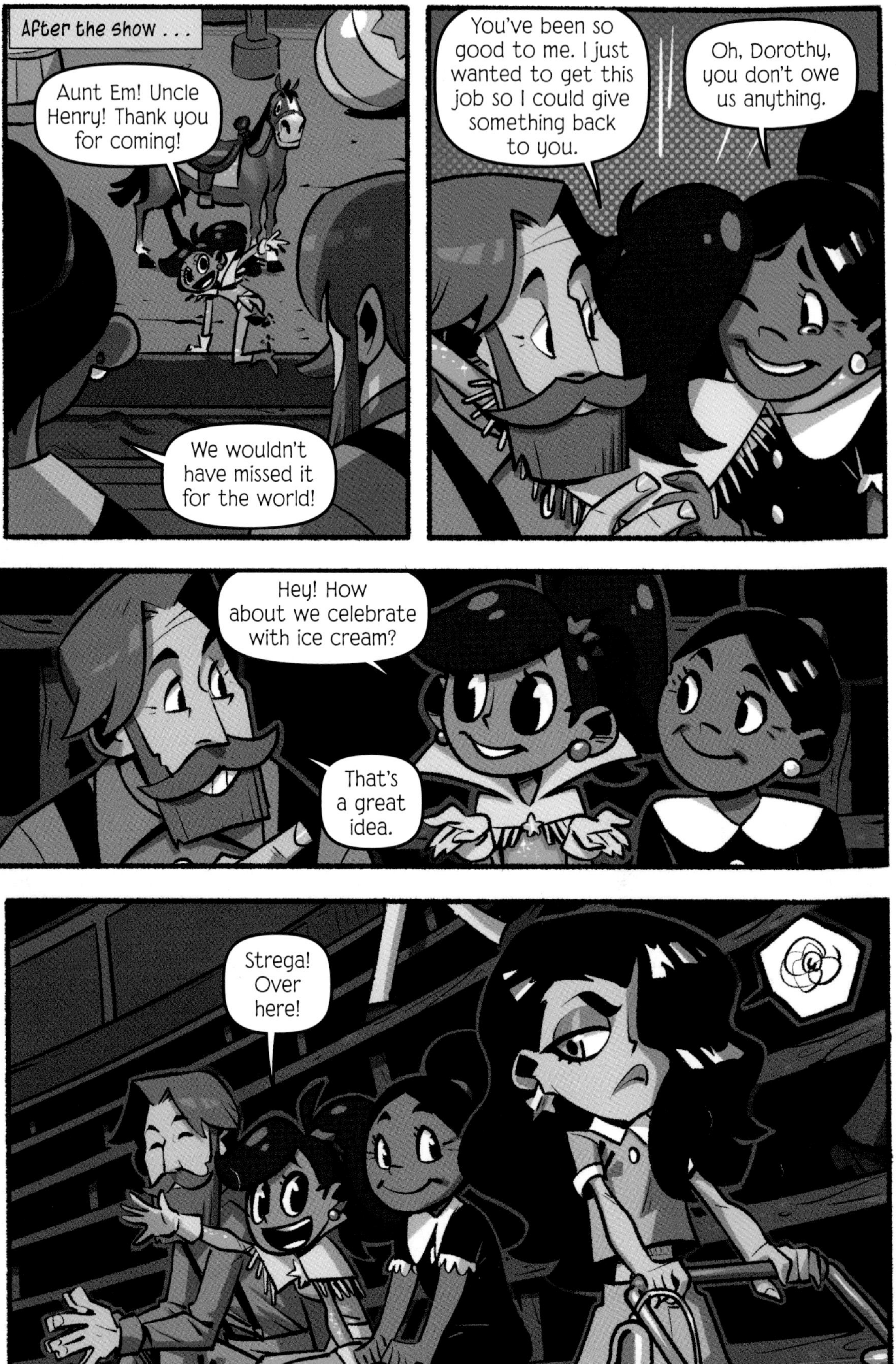
After the show . . .
Aunt Em! Uncle Henry! Thank you for coming!
We wouldn't have missed it for the world!
You've been so good to me. I just wanted to get this job so I could give something back to you.
Oh, Dorothy, you don't owe us anything.
Hey! How about we celebrate with ice cream?
That's a great idea.
Strega! Over here!

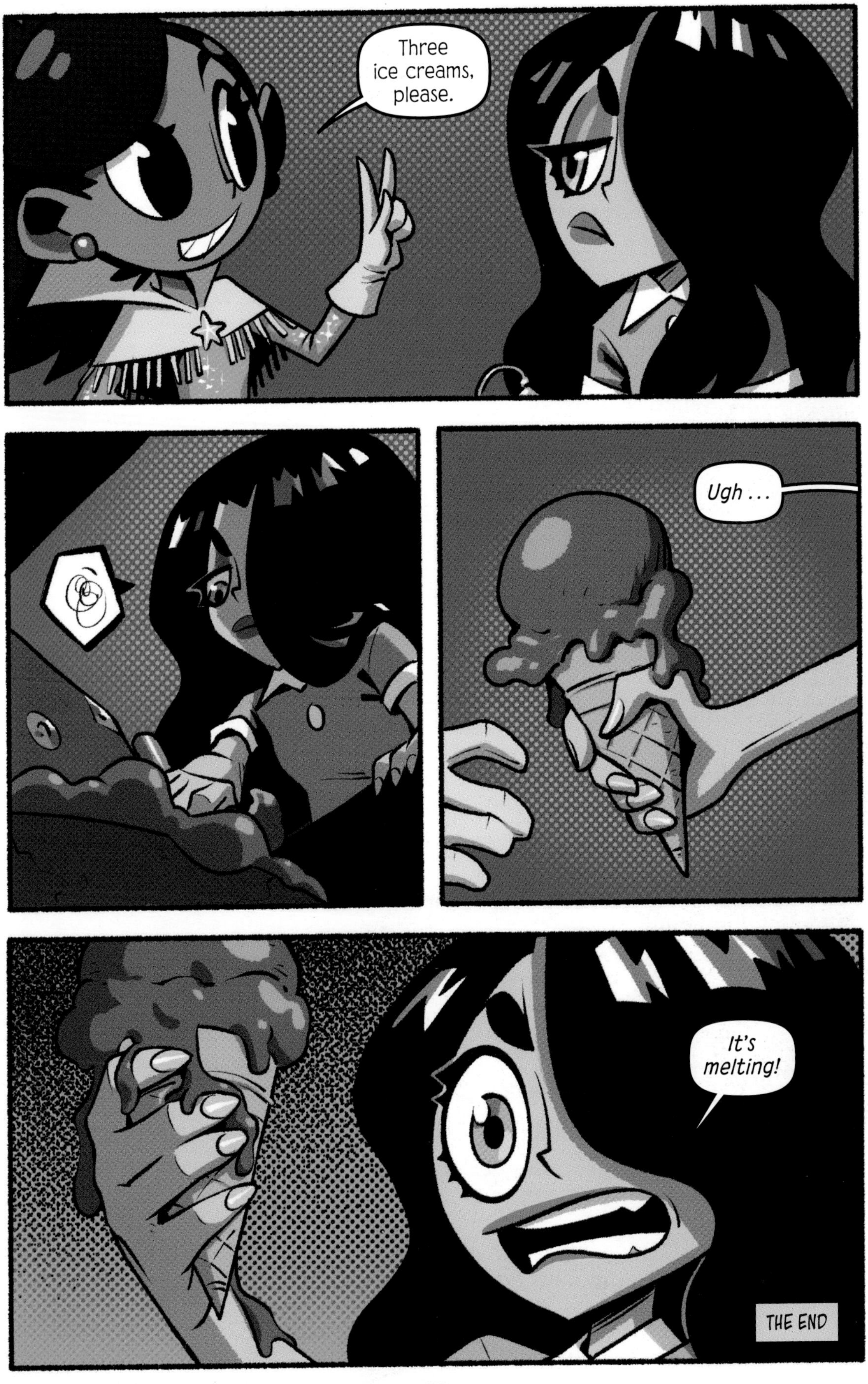
Three ice creams, please.
Ugh . . .
It's melting!
THE END

ALL ABOUT THE ORIGINAL STORY!

The Wonderful Wizard of Oz is a novel written by American author L. Frank Baum in 1900. Although the original doesn't take place in a circus, Dorothy still gets swept up into a colorful and captivating world.

The story starts on Dorothy's farm in Kansas. A cyclone strikes and lifts up Dorothy's house, taking the girl and her dog, Toto, with it. The house finally sets down in a strange land. A group of small people and the Good Witch of the North greet Dorothy and Toto. They tell Dorothy that her house fell on the Wicked Witch of the East, and now the witch's magical silver shoes belong to her.

But Dorothy just wants to go back home. She follows the Yellow Brick Road to the Emerald City in order to ask a wizard named Oz for help. Along the way, she meets three others who want to see Oz too. The Scarecrow wants a brain, the Tin Woodman wants a heart, and the Lion wants courage. After overcoming many challenges on their trip, they finally reach the Emerald City—only Oz won't help them unless they kill the Wicked Witch of the West!

The powerful witch knows the four are coming, so she sends her Winged Monkeys to stop them. Dorothy is kidnapped and forced to work in the witch's castle. When the witch steals one of Dorothy's silver shoes, the girl angrily throws a bucket of water on her. This defeats the witch—the water melts her into a pile of goo!

The four friends return to Oz to get their rewards, but the hot air balloon that's supposed to take Dorothy home flies off without her. Luckily, the good witch Glinda knows another way to travel. Dorothy just needs to use her magical silver shoes! Dorothy knocks her heels together three times and tells the shoes to take her to Aunt Em.

A **FAR OUT** GUIDE TO THE STORY'S WESTERN TWISTS!

Dorothy's magical silver shoes have been swapped out for lucky silver spurs!

In the original, Toto is Dorothy's little dog. Here, he is Dorothy's horse.

This time around, the villain isn't the Wicked Witch of the West. It's Strega West, a 13-year-old girl who's an archer and a trickster.

The great and terrible Oz is a peddler from Omaha who lives in the Emerald City. The Wiz Kid is a showman who runs the traveling Emerald Circus of Oz.

VISUAL QUESTIONS

Strega's word balloon has a squiggle inside it, not text. How would you read it out loud? What emotions do you think it expresses?

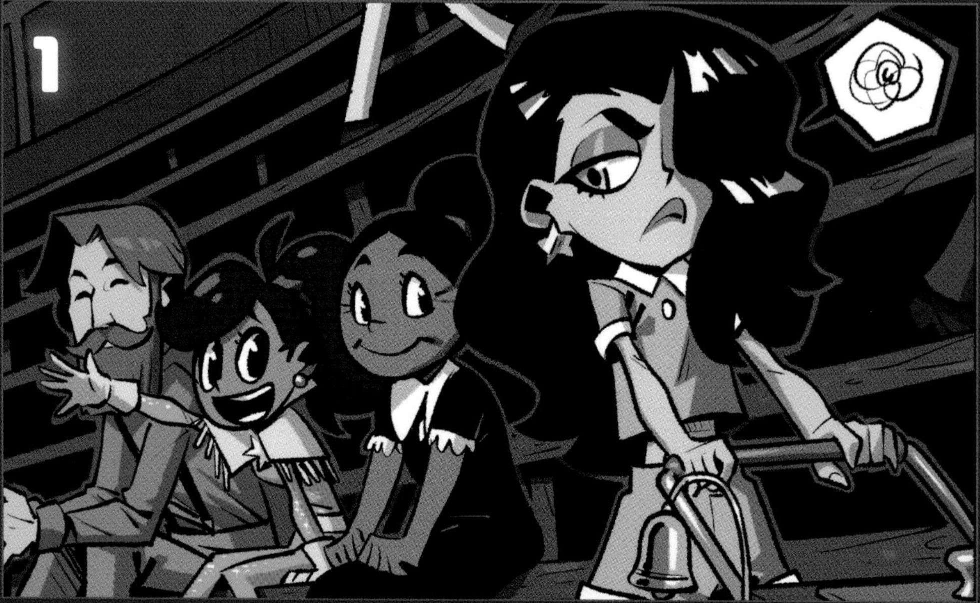
1

Graphic novels can pack a lot of info into a small amount of space. Write out what happens during Strega's audition, and be sure to make it exciting! (If you need help, turn to pages 21–23.)

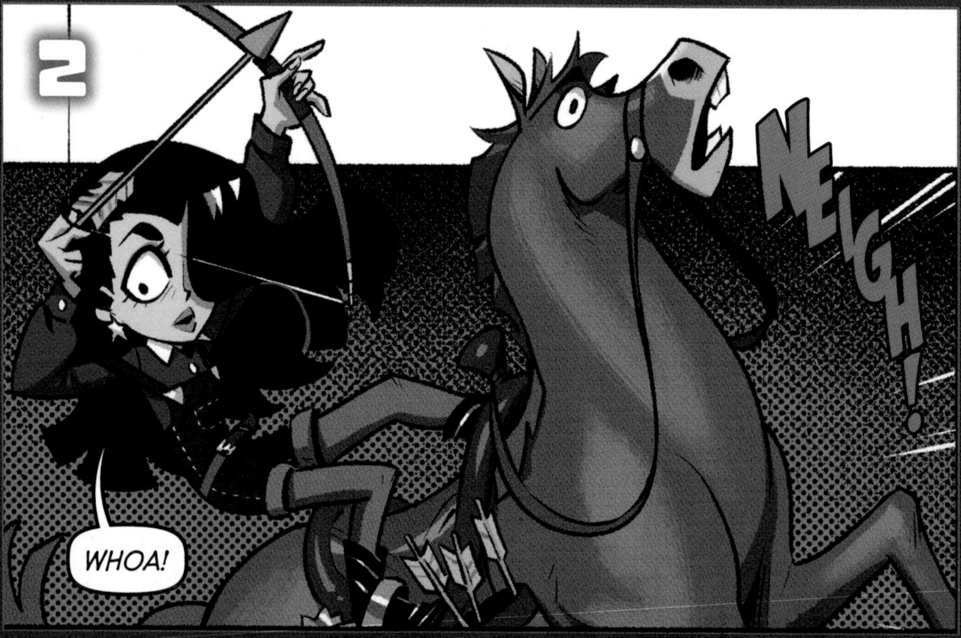
2
NEIGH!
WHOA!

Why do you think the artist drew the characters' eyes big and shiny here? Describe their feelings at this moment.

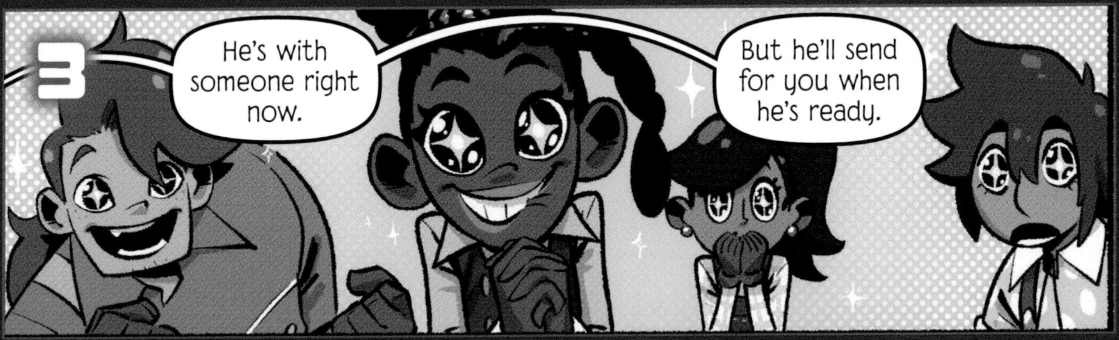
3
He's with someone right now.
But he'll send for you when he's ready.

Were you surprised that Strega stole Dorothy's silver spurs? Why or why not? Look back through and find two moments in the art and text that hint at her plan.

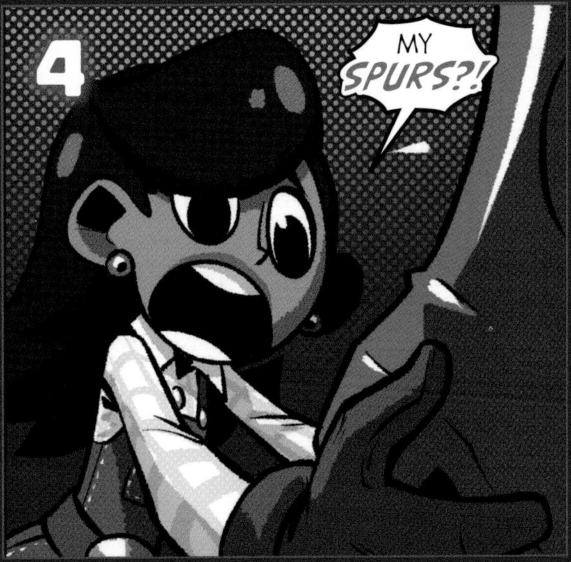
4
MY SPURS?!

These panels are slanted instead of rectangular. How does their shape match what's happening in the story? How would it feel different if they were normal boxes?

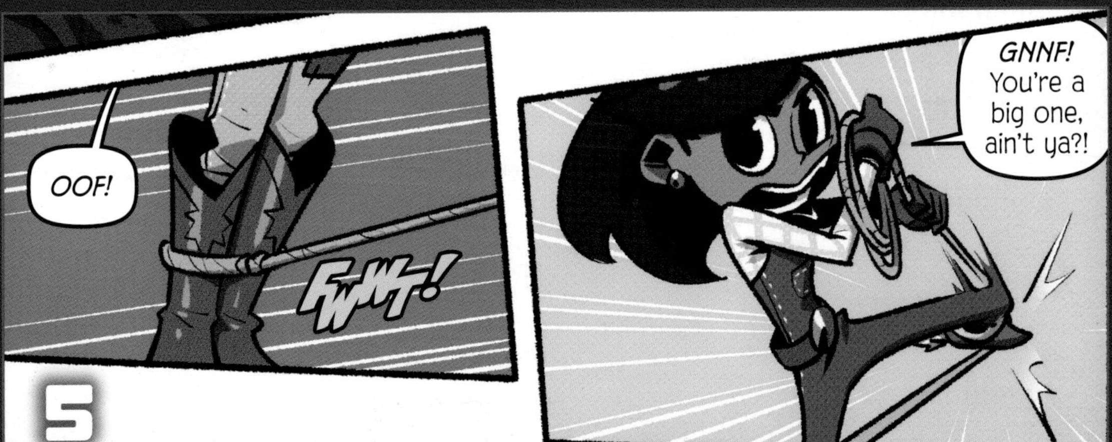
OOF!
GNNF! You're a big one, ain't ya?!
5

AUTHOR

Erica Schultz is an American comic book writer, letterer, and editor who has been active in the industry since 2008. She has worked on comics production, background art, and ink and color assists for Neal Adams' Continuity Studios. Erica also teamed up with artist Vicente Alcázar to create the award-winning creator-owned series M3, published by Vices Press. Her other accolades include writing Xena: Warrior Princess and Charmed for Dynamite Entertainment; editing *Bingo Love* for Image Comics, which was a 2019 GLAAD Media Award nominee; and being a founding editor of RISE: Comics Against Bullying.

ILLUSTRATOR

Omar Lozano lives in Monterrey, Mexico. He has always been crazy for illustration and is constantly on the lookout for awesome things to draw. In his free time, he watches lots of movies, reads fantasy and sci-fi books, and draws! Omar has worked for Marvel Comics, DC Comics, IDW, Dark Horse Comics, Capstone, and several other publishing companies.

GLOSSARY

acrobat (AK-ruh-bat)—a person who does jumping, tumbling, balancing, and other similar acts

archer (AR-chuhr)—a person who shoots a bow and arrow

audition (aw-DISH-uhn)—an event where people show off their talents in hopes of getting a place in a show or group; also, to try out

cyclone (SY-clohn)—a powerful, fast-spinning column of air; also called a tornado

impress (im-PRESS)—to cause someone to think highly of you, usually through your actions

lasso (LAS-oh)—a rope formed into a loop; a lasso is mostly used by cowboys to catch animals but can also be used to do tricks

obliged (uh-BLIJED)—if you are obliged to someone, they have done a nice thing for you and you owe them a nice act back

perform (pur-FORM)—to carry out a skilled action or activity in front of others

routine (roo-TEEN)—a series of skillful acts that have been planned out and practiced ahead of time

spur (SPUR)—a pointed metal object worn on the boots of some horse riders

trinket (TRING-kit)—a small object that isn't worth much

OLD FAVORITES. NEW SPINS.